Santa and Anna Christmas Cookie Crash

California Dreams

Talya Blaine

ISBN ebook: 978-1-959336-16-7

ISBN audiobook: 978-1-959336-17-4

ISBN paperback 978-1-959336-18-1

To the subscribers at the other end of my email newsletters.
Thank you for being there.

Contents

prologue: attachment issue

In the dream, she skated a wide figure-eight, arms stretched out like wings, gliding free. Cool air rushed past her face; her cashmere scarf fluttered. Blake and the kids waved from the far side of the huge rink, not far from the enormous tree. It might be Rockefeller Center on Christmas Eve, but somehow the four of them had the ice to themselves. Thousands of tiny golden lights adorned the skyscraper spruce, glittering like stars in the Manhattan twilight—indigo, fuchsia, and violet backlit the winter sky—giving her the feeling she was fly...

Suddenly, a loud metallic crack sliced the air, and the blade of her skate broke clear off, sending her tumbling down to the ice. She spun on her back like a top, then careened into the side wall with a thud.

The kids raced over. Blake took his sweet time.

"What happened?" he asked when he finally reached them.

"I fell," she started to say but got distracted by the bottom of her bladeless skate, trying to understand what happened. There were no holes, no metal plates, no sign anything had once been attached.

"Yeah, I got that much, Anna." Arms crossed, he huffed a few feet above her, his lips chapped and dry from the cold. He looked around for the kids, who somehow were now safely out of earshot. "Enough with the sarcasm," he added. "We're not married anymore; you don't have to be a bitch."

And then—thank you, Christmas miracle—he skated off and disappeared.

From the edge of her field of vision, a rink security guard glided over and helped her up. The bell on the tip of his floppy yellow and green elf hat jing-a-linged as he dusted ice shavings off her coat and offered his arm in support.

Once she collected herself and got a good look at the man under the hat, she noticed he was quite handsome and that it was very pleasant to watch him in motion. The muscles of his chest and biceps flexed beneath his tight black sweater. His thick dark hair bounced. Heat stirred in her body, somewhere deep and low. The space between them hummed with electricity; the air no longer felt cold. His blue eyes sparkled like a tropical lagoon, and they remained fixed on her when he asked, "Can I take you home?"

Only it wasn't her Costa Mesa townhouse they went to, it was the back room of her bakery. The order board hung on the wall; the laminated, handwritten recipes hung from the edge of the shelves. Tall racks of cooling cookie sheets waited beside the steel counter. Wide aquamarine boxes, with *Anna's Bakery of Cookies* printed on the lids, surrounded them in neat piles. When he spied the small loveseat in her office, he picked her up as if she were a bride and carried her over the threshold. "What do you think, Anna? Is it alright if I stay?"

She looked into the mirror beside the office door to see if this was real. The reflection was theirs alright—her brown eyes, wavy chestnut hair, hips whose curves gained extra padding this time of year. He stood behind her, started to unwrap her scarf as if she were a present, pressed his lips to her neck for a single kiss.

"Is this okay?" he asked, meeting her gaze in the glass.

"Yes," she told him with a sigh as she leaned back against his broad chest. "Yes, it's more than okay; I definitely think you should stay."

Chapter 1
best laid... plan

If *only*. The dream from early this morning with the sexy Santa faded as Anna peeked out from the back room. The line snaked around the long glass case, unfurling like gift ribbon to the front door. But Siena and Reef, a.k.a. Arthur, her loyal and unflappable employees, had this. The white pom poms of their Santa hats wagged as they chatted with customers and took orders, filling the bakery's signature green boxes with cookies from the case.

Although Anna didn't personally feel so much of it this morning, the Christmas-spirit meter hummed in the high zone—from the excited chatter and holiday wishes she overheard to the carols playing softly in the background. Cedar roping with dangling red and green ornaments and twinkling lights ran along the soffits, and giant Coulter pine cones—courtesy of the backyard tree at the old house on Balboa Island—hung from the ceiling, each at different heights.

While customers buzzed in the front and the mixer whirred behind her, Anna decorated the next sheet of sugar cookies for the special orders. Since the shop was so small and she was a one-woman baking operation, at Christmas she simplified her repertoire, kept the offerings bare bones, and focused on the icing decoration. No complicated dough recipes with time-consuming curlicues of zest or chocolate shavings, just delicious, buttery sugar cookies in various shapes and sizes: palm trees with Christmas ornaments framed with an orange- and lavender-streaked sunset, snowflakes, Hollywood stars, Santas on surfboards, and Rudolphs with big antlers waving from the driver's side of a sports car.

And sailboats. With holiday lights dabbed with sparkly, edible frosting for a real estate developer in Corona del Mar. His fancy yacht won an award for its lights in the Newport boat parade last December, and when his assistant couldn't decide what kind of cookies to order, these were what Anna designed. One by one, she dotted each tiny bulb with the tip of her piping bag and then with her tweezers she added an extra touch, a minuscule flake of food-safe gold-leaf foil.

That dream. She lifted the canvas bag and for just a quick moment closed her eyes to savor the memory. The recollection was slipping, although she tried hard—*mm, yes, very hard*—to hold onto it. Blake being a jerk was more or less exactly like reality, but that she would finally have amazing sex with a gorgeous, sweet guy? That was about as likely in real life as Santa coming down her chimney.

No pun intended. She did not have a romantic prospect to save her life. Or, for that matter, a fireplace.

Over the hum of the mixer, her phone jingled and vibrated against the steel counter. The sound of the "We Wish You a Merry Christmas" alert made her smile. It wasn't her usual tone, which meant Carli must have changed it as a joke. Anna shrugged away the pang of sadness, of longing, as she glanced over at the screen. Speaking of Carli, it was her, texting from New York with a photo of an elaborate department store Christmas window display. Anna tapped the image, squinted to make out the vignette, and let out a genuine laugh. Now *that* was a serious elf-bakery operation.

Good luck with all your cookie orders today, mom!

With voice commands, Anna texted back.

Thanks, honey! How's New York?

Great! But I miss you.

Anna started to dictate, "I miss you too," but before she could finish Carli followed with a selfie modeling a not-so-appropriate-for-a-fifteen-year-old dress. Anna could see from the thick gold frame around the floor mirror and the sharply dressed personal shopper trying to stay out of the photo that it was an exclusive department store, a place Anna never would have taken her.

Blake's thumb cut into the corner of the picture, right by the white price tag. He probably had turned the tag around and held it in place to make sure Anna could see it. It wasn't paranoia on her part; since the divorce, that was totally the type of thing he would do.

But Anna wasn't going to squint this time to see the dollar amount; she would not play into his battle-for-the-kids'-affection games and also, she didn't want to know.

Let him try to earn the kids' respect by buying them expensive stuff. She would not get aggravated. Repeat: She would not get aggravated. As she kept reminding herself since he picked Carli up yesterday to visit Ben at college in

New York City, Blake was giving the kids a nice winter vacation, doing Christmas in the Big Apple. A picture-perfect, postcard-ready Christmas in Manhattan with Madison, his pretty, young new wife—"new" referring strictly to the recency of their nuptials, not how long they had been screwing around behind Anna's back.

Not. Aggravated.

With a deep, cleansing screw-Blake breath—not *that* kind of screw-Blake—she focused on decorating tray after tray.

When she was done with the batch, she set the piping bag down and methodically row by row eyed each cookie on the sheets for any slip-ups that needed correcting.

Not bad. Only a couple of wayward drips of icing here and there that she carefully removed with her food pick.

By mid-morning, the courier service took off with most of the orders and the flow of incoming customers slowed. Once Reef had helped the last person in line, Anna locked the front door and turned the sign to closed. Reef got out the vacuum and the mop, while Siena followed Anna into the back and helped her fill the rest of the deep boxes with layers of cookies and carefully-placed dividers.

"These are so amazing," Siena said while the two of them packed the orders. "You have a real knack, Anna. Each one is like a miniature work of art."

"Without you and Reef on the front lines, I wouldn't be able to do it. Once we get this last dozen into the box, you two should go. It's been a long morning, and you should start your holiday already." The Christmas Eve shift was the bakery's most intense—super-busy and starting so early they joked about how they ought to camp in the back room the night before.

Not that three people could fit back there if they weren't on their feet.

Anna didn't mind. The shop was tiny, but it was hers—relying on her artistry and creativity, her spin on recipes from her mother—and she loved it. With the exception of Siena and Reef's part-time help, she had built the business on her own. Still, as much as she loved this place, she was looking forward to tonight after the gala, when she could take off her dress, let down her hair, fall onto the couch and watch one of her favorite movies.

Low-conflict Christmas romances with couples and families that practiced the art of compromise, with reliably optimistic endings. She had been squirreling them onto her streaming watchlist since Thanksgiving. They were her guilty pleasure and, more to the point, her solace, her vicarious Christmas spirit at the holiday, when neither the kids nor her mom were with her.

"I swore I wouldn't admit this to another soul," Siena said as they loaded the final boxes, "but the only invitation I got for tonight was from my Aunt Betty and Uncle Burt, and they tend to hit the hot buttered rum pretty hard." She pretended to shudder at the thought. "It's not pretty."

"No, that doesn't sound good, although...hot buttered rum." Anna smiled and mocked a shrug.

"I know, right? But it's a gut bomb. You have to know when to stop. And therein lies the problem. So I can easily help you with the deliveries and tell them tomorrow that I stopped by last night. They'll be asleep by, oh, four thirty; they'll hardly remember whether I did or not."

"That sounds like it might be a good course of action," Anna said in jest. "It's nice of you to offer to help but, really, it's been a long day and I can manage on my own. Besides, I don't want either of you to get burned out. I'll really need your help when—I mean, *if*," Anna corrected so as not to set anyone up for disappointment, least of all herself, "we open a second location next year."

"ABC number two—that would be so awesome, lady. By the way, who are you taking tonight to the Angels' gala?"

"Oh...I don't know," she said and moved her pursed lips side to side as if contemplating the choices. "I couldn't decide which hunky Prince Charming to ask, so I settled on just me, myself, and I."

Siena's hopeful expression turned sad. Sad for Anna. Sad as in, pity. "You can't attend the Orange County Christmas Angels' secret-invitation gala alone. Let me go with you, or take Reef. You should have a cheering section there. You're going to win, I know it."

"That's sweet of you," Anna said, "but honestly, I don't mind going solo. I'm serious—you two need to have down time. But"—she held up two crossed fingers— "please do send good vibes out into the universe for us to win."

* * *

Good vibes. An image of the man in her dream shimmied to life and just as quickly evaporated.

Siena looked as if she wanted to say more. Anna guessed it was a question about taking not an employee or a friend but an actual date, as in a real, live single man. Which Anna didn't want to answer because she didn't do real, live-man dates.

"I almost forgot—" Anna pointed toward the cubbyhole that was her office. "There's an envelope for you and for Reef on my desk. Take them before you go." She hoped that didn't sound dismissive; she was grateful for Siena's offers to help, but things were usually easier when you took care of them alone. "Merry Christmas."

"Thanks, boss. Merry Christmas." Siena stifled what looked like it was about to be a sigh, and then she smiled. Sort of. It was more one of those I'm-disappointed-on-your-behalf smiles. "Try to do something fun and nice for yourself, Anna. You work really hard and, well, don't forget that it's Christmas tomorrow."

She didn't say it to Siena because most people didn't understand, but for Anna, work *was* fun. Work was safe. Work meant security. Unlike Blake, work didn't throw life-changing curveballs to whack her and her life with the kids right in the side of the head.

Anna leaned in to give her a hug. "I will. Now take your envelope and go home—or to Aunt Betty and Uncle Burt's while they're still standing."

Anna closed the last aqua-colored lid and placed the box carefully on one of the piles just as Reef came into the back. "All set," he said, pointing toward the front of the shop. "Floor's wet. Don't slip. I'm heading to Southside—with the winds today there's awesome wave. But before I take off, I'll load the van." Now, he pointed toward the back door.

"I won't slip, don't worry, and I'll load it myself. Have a great time." It was touching how concerned he and Siena were. For a brief moment, she wondered what they were like ten years ago, and if her own kids—Carli mostly, since she was younger—would turn into similarly kind, engaged, responsible adults. Kind, engaged, responsible adults who might joke about quirky relatives but who, Anna knew, would faithfully and good-heartedly go visit anyway.

She reached around the wall to her office and grabbed the printout and pencil from her desk. That was one advantage of a shop the size of a postage-stamp. Although if she got the Angels' investment, she would make sure Anna's Bakery of Cookies number two was larger, with a cool, clean marble-topped island in the center of the back room to provide much-needed workspace.

She said a silent *please* to the Angels, who had surprised her with an invite to the gala four weeks ago to the day. Only Siena and Reef and the kids, all of whom Anna had sworn to secrecy, knew she had applied for venture funding back in June. And that her presence had been requested at their Christmas gala, which meant she was a finalist.

The elegant invitation had been delivered in a thin green box and tied with stretchy gold ribbon so it looked like a Christmas gift. Which was exactly what it would be for the winning business, a lucky, promising local mom-and-pop operation the Angels wanted to invest in and help to expand.

From the list of V. I. P. orders on the pages in her hand, she cross-checked the name and address on the printed label on the short side of each rectangular box in the lower left-hand corner. With a final tick next to the last name on the list, the extra-special orders were ready to go.

This was her thing. Every Christmas Eve, she hand-delivered orders to her very best clients, the ones nestled snug in their cliffside Coast Highway homes. They were actors and politicians, surgeons and philanthropists, influencers and socialites, a rock star, a prince, two tech billionaires. It was her way of saying thank you for their business and their loyalty. And just like Anna knew they didn't wear the same outfit to more than one event, she never designed them the same cookies twice.

Her clients paid handsomely—for her originality, her dependability, her reputation. They ordered repeatedly for their special events, referred their friends and colleagues often. Without them and their trust, Anna's Bakery of Cookies wouldn't have grown from nothing to thriving these last four years of her rocky, post-divorce life.

Next, she double-checked the big order for the children's hospital Christmas luncheon, to which she donated cookies every year. *All set.* She grabbed her keys from the hook on the wall and ran outside to re-park the van in the alley right by the back door. Once she loaded all the cookie boxes, she would run back in and quickly change into her dress.

Inside once more, she dropped the key fob in her pocket and shut off the bakery lights, wiped a last couple of crumbs off the counter. With the back door propped open, one at a time she took the top three boxes off a pile on the counter, careful to keep them level. Crouching, she shimmied them onto her forearms. Three boxes at once was her limit, her rule; she never risked an accident by trying to carry more.

Outside, the air was cool, but the sun blazed hot. She set the boxes on the van's cargo floor and turned them so the short sides rested against the grate behind the front seats. Then she hurried around to the driver's side to blast the air conditioning. Iced cookies, rays of sun, the glass window a focusing prism. That was the last thing she would need today, for the cookies' icing to melt.

The radio came on as soon as she started the motor. "Folks, Santa's in for a bumpy ride over SoCal tonight," said the deep voice of a practiced male announcer. "Traffic and a wind alert for the Santa Anas, along with the rest of the holiday weather, coming up next."

She didn't wait to hear the forecast. The traffic she would check on the van's GPS and after the deliveries, she was only going to the gala, which was taking place in the country club ballroom, safely inside. And then after the gala, she was headed straight home. A shower, yoga pants, TV. She might shift positions to reach the bag of microwave popcorn or to exchange goodnight texts with the kids or to fetch a pint of ice cream from the freezer, but that was all. The wind warnings didn't matter to her plans; they were one-hundred percent weather-proof.

* * *

The wind gusted warm and dry, carrying the scent of creosote bushes from the desert as she headed back toward the bakery door to grab the next three boxes. The hem of her chef's jacket flapped, and her eyes squinched shut by instinct to protect from a flurry of sand and dust. The Santa Ana winds were forceful; when they blew, they blew hard. It was good the hospital Christmas party wasn't happening in the outdoor courtyard. She imagined a rogue gust lifting cookies off the table, her race car Rudolfs and surfing Santas swirling in the blustery air.

Once inside again, she kicked the small rubber wedge doorstop out of the way to swap it for a weightier bag of flour.

Her phone buzzed and jingled with another text alert, and she slid it out of her pocket. A photo expanded on her screen, a picture from the kids on the ice at Rockefeller Center. Ben was giving Carli a noogie as the two of them grinned in front of the massive tree.

For a brief second, Anna's mind flashed to the hunk at the rink in her dreams. The phone buzzed and jangled a second alert, and she shook the man-thoughts away as she tried to think of how to respond. Upbeat-mom was the tone she strived for, rather than angry-at-Blake that she and the kids were apart.

> Fun!! Is it cold?

> Freeeeezing. And OMG mom, it just started to snow!

> Right on time! #whiteChristmas!

At her hashtag, Anna could picture Carli roll her eyes.

> We're on Fifth Avenue. Right by the Spiralo store. Mom, can I get a Spiralo watch?

Anna tensed. Carli was relentless when she wanted something. That bleeping smartwatch practically cost more than what the bakery earned in a week.

> We've talked about this (a lot!) No Spiralo watch.

> But why? It does everything. It has A. I.

> You're 15. You have a bright, young, healthy brain. You don't need A. I.

> #badmom #foreheadL #doesntunderstand

> #iknow,worstmomEVER

> #seriously #justplainmean

Anna waited a few seconds because she sensed the change in tone. She knew her daughter. Carli's disposition generally was kind and sweet, so she would need a moment to wind up. But then, Anna held her breath, because her mercurial teenager also could hurl a wicked sucker punch.

The three bubbles blinked and faded, and here it was, a page straight from Blake's playbook:

#bitter

Since the divorce, it had gotten harder and harder to temper that biting edge of his personality and his negative influence. Especially when the kids—again, mainly Carli, since Ben was older and away at college—spent longer than a day or two with him. Anna could sometimes hear him in Carli's voice and texts, see his disdain in her eyes when she came home to Anna. Home to real life, to structure and rules and stability. Home to the parent who was willing to say, *no*.

Sometimes Anna felt as if she were losing Carli to him. Temporarily, Anna hoped, but it stung. The kids were the center of her life; every single decision, every action she took, she contemplated with them at heart—what they needed, how to encourage them to grow into good people, how to keep them fed and clothed and safe and secure and...

The lack of bubbles on the phone screen told her Carli was done going on about the watch and conveying all the ways Anna was letting her down—at least for right now.

How many times had they talked about why Carli didn't need such an expensive toy? Anna hoped she would come to appreciate the differences between Anna's and Blake's parenting approaches as she got older. Anna would never do anything to poison the kids' relationship with him, never say anything bad behind his back. So many times she had almost let something accidentally slip about his affair, but she would not tell them. Maybe they suspected, or possibly Blake would share, but no matter how hard it might be to bite her tongue about his misdeeds, it would not come from Anna.

Before she put the phone back in her pocket, she checked the clock. Thanks to the texting, she was running behind. Six boxes remained on the counter. She needed to hustle if she was going to deliver like she promised.

It was only a few feet from the bakery's back door to the van—she could carry them all, make an exception to her steadfast rule for this one super-important, urgent time.

* * *

James stood at the bathroom mirror and pulled the strap of the Santa beard over his head before putting on the wig. He tugged and straightened one after the other, put the glue on the mustache, carefully centered it above his top lip, and pressed it to his skin.

He did the same with the wide, white bushy eyebrows, and then picked up the glasses from beside the sink. The fake gold wire-rimmed frames that came in the deluxe costume kit were a little tight at the temples, but the hospital party was only two hours. *No big deal.* Rubbing some of the blush that came in the package on the tip of his nose, he leaned closer to the mirror.

Not bad.

But damn it, that the belly padding hadn't arrived on time really bummed him out. The tracking webpage said it was on the truck and out for delivery two days ago, and his inquiry yesterday had gone unanswered. He wanted that belly for authenticity's sake, so he would really look like a Santa.

But as his mind reviewed the past, he considered how

Dr. Washingtonn, a hospital therapist he had seen, might have held a different opinion. When they knew each other back then, she might have pursed her lips in thought and slowly nodded—he could picture it as if she were standing in the bathroom doorway behind him. If it was one of their talking days, she might have asked if his fixation on the belly padding might hold a deeper meaning, if it could be because he wanted some kind of extra cushioning or protection, a suit of armor of sorts.

And he would immediately, without any thought, have huffed out a snorty laugh and waved it off, as if the suggestion were silly.

He wondered if she was working today, and if she might stop by the party. Not that he wanted to talk about anything, more like he just wanted to show her. But her stopping by was unlikely—he remembered that from before, how she always seemed to be tucked away in her office at the far end of that wing. The only thing beyond her door was a window wall that looked out onto a peaceful court-yard garden with a gurgling fountain.

He collected the costume packaging and headed toward the kitchen, where he dumped it in the cardboard box on the floor that he used as a recycling bin.

At the coat closet by the front door, the wire hangers clinked as he pulled down the Santa coat and put it on. His windbreaker was the only thing left in the closet—the thing he really should wear today considering how the Santa Anas had whipped up a little while ago. But the windproof jacket wouldn't fit over the Santa coat and, besides, what's a few strong gusts?

No big deal.

He squared his shoulders and inhaled a deep breath, reminding himself he had volunteered to do this; he needed to do this; he had promised to do this. It was only a couple of hours. *No big deal.*

And then he would reward himself for a job hopefully well done by picking up tacos al pastor carryout for supper. He would eat at the rickety bistro table on the small apartment balcony and nurse a beer, while trying to imagine a better view than the parking lot of the big shopping center. By ten o'clock, he would go to bed so he could get up for work at five on Christmas morning.

It was a relief, work, starting early and putting in long hours, covering for the other chef when she wanted to take time off. Work meant less time to ruminate. Less headspace to fill with memories. Less time to make small talk with Claire when she would, like every year, call later today or tomorrow.

Christmas Day and his birthday, the two days she reached out. Not much different than their sex life during the time their disintegrating marriage sputtered its final breaths.

Work meant less time to wish for things that could not actually come true.

But anyway. It was too late to back out of the Santa gig. Again, he remembered the Santa who visited Noah when he was at Children's and the rare, high-watt smile that had blossomed on his little face. James could not disappoint the young patients today. Some might be at Children's for a few days, others might not make it home, but it didn't matter what their situations were. He had told the hospital he would play Santa today and committed to making a few kids smile for a measly two-hour Christmas party. So nothing— *nothing*—was going to stop him, neither memories nor waylaid belly padding.

A loud knock on the front door startled him out of his

blue trance. He grabbed the knob with the dingy ring around the trim plate and turned it.

"Hi, uh…"

"James," he said. "I'm James." He extended his right hand but quickly realized the guy's was occupied, holding a cardboard delivery box.

"Ernest," he said, offering the carton. "It was sitting outside my front door. Delivery guy must have left it there by mistake. I thought you might need it, being it's Christmas Eve and all."

"I do need it—like, today, like right now. Thanks a lot for bringing it over."

"Glad to help," Ernest replied. He looked over James' shoulder at the piles of moving boxes and made a face like he might be confused. "I haven't been here that long myself, moved a few months back from Visalia."

James just nodded. He had spent a few months in the Central Valley, working as a cook in a nursing home near Stockton, but he didn't want to get caught up in conversation in case Ernest was a talker.

"If you need a hand unpacking, I'm off from the job until New Year's, and I have a truck—I can help you bring stuff home from the stores. Save you the delivery fees. And everything always goes on sale on the 26th. There's a furniture place on…"

"Thanks, man. I'm good," James said. "Work is really busy right now—I'm pulling extra shifts, but I might hit you up when it slows down."

And I might not.

"Okay, well, the offer stands. I'm in 4E," he said, pointing downward in the direction of the stairs and to the left.

"Thank you, Ernest in 4E. You saved the day with this."

James shook the box, anticipation rising as if he were a kid on Christmas morning. *Yes.*

The second Ernest started down the stairs, James closed the door and unpacked the box, took off his Santa coat and shirt, put the harness with the molded silicone belly on.

He waddled back to the bathroom mirror, making a mental note to practice a more natural gait. The padding was larger and heavier than he expected based on the costume shop website description. It hung low even on his six-foot frame. He imagined Dr. Washingtonn by his shoulder again because the fake gut did give an immediate air of legitimacy and the confidence boost he lacked.

He looked in the mirror one last time. *You got this.*

He re-dressed and hurried out, pulling up the bus schedule and route on his phone. Even with the considerable walk, the bus would be faster than taking the car like he would on a typical workday. This, he hadn't missed about the whole L. A. metro area, the ten-plus-lane I-405 parking lot.

He widened his fingers to expand the map until the smallest streets appeared as faint gray lines. Great, it looked like he could cut through an alley behind a row of shops to shave off a few minutes' time.

He patted his big belly, re-adjusted the belt buckle for the third time in as many minutes to help keep it in place. A smile plinked the corner of his mouth as he locked the front door behind him, slow-waddle-jogged down the stairs and out the building's front door. Left toward the bus stop and—*no way!*—he grabbed hold of his Santa hat as a whipping gust of wind almost blew it off.

Chapter 2
the way the cookie crumbles

Anna's phone jingled and buzzed again inside her back pocket, and as much as she wanted to communicate with the kids, this time it would have to wait. Besides, it was probably more photos, taken at some famous place where Blake and Madison would want to stop to buy the kids a cup of hot cocoa just to say they'd been there. Anna could see in her mind's eye the glistening hand-whipped cream, the curls of the cinnamon stick, the dusting of cocoa powder, all styled and social-media ready.

She bent her knees to bring her forearms counter-height and shimmied the cookie boxes forward. Carefully, she rose and went outside to slide them into the back of the van. The wind gusted again, and she recoiled at the force, turning her face away.

A few doors down some guy dressed as Santa was walking fast, his big belly jiggling, his head angled down toward his phone.

The wind gusted again long and loud, and instinctively her eyes flinched shut. She took a deep breath and started to count to ten while she kept them closed to protect them. And then it was hard to tell, but it sounded like from very, very close up Santa suddenly yelled, "No! Damn it. *Oh, fudge!*"

Her eyes flew open as the impact knocked her back, but she caught her balance and didn't fall. The long boxes—*no!* They were a different story. In slow motion, the top three angled forward. She pitched back to rein them in. One leg flew out in front of her to balance. But the reflex was too late. The boxes had the advantage of momentum and she winced, watching in slow-motion horror as one by one they slid off the pile and hit the sidewalk.

Thunk. Thunk. Thunk. The dented lids bounced off, and cookies, broken cookies, spilled out.

"Sorry! Sorry! Are you alright?" Santa asked, as she yanked her arm from his grasp.

"I'm not alright! Look!" She pointed to the ground. You're a real..." *Jerk! Asshole!* "I can't believe... Why weren't you watching... Geez, what kind of idiot runs around outside on the street in a Santa costume? Couldn't you change, like a normal person, when you get to your"—she moved her head since she was not letting go of those other three boxes to wave one hand around frantically like instinct would have dictated—"your...destination?"

"I was trying to see where I was when something blew into my eye, and"—he was holding his enormous beer belly with one hand and, eww, just eww, with the other hand he adjusted his big belt—"at the same time the padding slipped. Sorry! Again."

He started to say something else, but she raised her hand to silence him. "Rhetorical questions," she said as she knelt to set the remaining boxes on the sidewalk for safety. On second thought, she lifted the boxes back up again so this clown wouldn't trip over them and do even more damage than he had already done.

He looked at her like she was nuts, which at least temporarily, she was. That might be why some distant part of her consciousness registered that his brief grip on her arm had felt firm and supportive and concerned, that the lips partially hidden under his mustache looked soft and full and had a nice shape, that the eyes behind his tiny oval frames conveyed an honestness she hadn't noticed in a man in a long time.

None of this was good; it only meant she must really be in some kind of shock and seriously out of her head.

"I am so sorry," he said more slowly and collected, his voice possessing a calm tone. He was finally done playing with his stupid belt, but he had the audacity to look down at his phone screen again. "Terribly sorry," he added, this time sounding rushed, "but I gotta' go."

Seriously? The guy slams into her, busts up her cookies, and he just...just waltzes off, goes on his merry effing way?

Wow, this male specimen made Blake look like the real Santa Claus.

"I'm very, very, very sorry," he called over his shoulder as he continued his saunter down the street. His voice faded but she could, unfortunately, still hear it. "Really very sorry."

Did he not learn anything just now? "Watch where you're going!" she screamed, but her voice dissolved into the wind.

Reason edged into her thoughts. It was an accident. He seemed genuine when he apologized. But he hadn't been paying attention; his face had been buried in...probably some porn on his mobile. And instead of helping her fix the shitstorm he caused, he left her standing here, cookies broken, alone.

Although "cookies" technically was not the right word to describe the bits and crumbs scattered on the sidewalk like snow.

* * *

James stopped for a second at the next corner, wiped his scratchy, tearing eye and tightened the belt yet again, checking to make sure the hat was still stuffed inside his pants pocket. That wind, holy moly. It was scary how sudden and strong the Santa Anas could blow.

It was also scary how angry that woman was. He hadn't experienced so much emotion on a woman's face, in a woman's eyes, since Claire had moved out. It might have been rotten of him to rush off just now but frankly that anger, such strong feelings, they unnerved him. And besides, he had somewhere important to be.

It only happened a minute ago, but he couldn't recall her hair style or her features now. It was as if his vision had narrowed like the aperture of a camera lens, letting in not light or lines or texture but *reaction*: disappointment, outrage at something he had done. One nanosecond he was trying to figure out back-roads directions on his phone; the next, he wondered what jabbed him in the eye, why the Santa belly suddenly heaved backward into his gut. An instant after that, *kapow! crash!* like a comic book text-balloon flare. When he stepped back, something had squished and flattened under his black boot.

He closed one eye now and tugged on the lid trying to free whatever particle was still poking his eyeball. At the touch of his own skin, he remembered how, right after their impact and in that split second of time before her anger exploded, he had felt a flash of... something.

Something.

What was it? Warmth? Wanting to take the boxes out of her arms and help her carry them? An affinity? *Attraction?* The blurry haze of memory began to sharpen. Her eyes— they were pretty. Big. Brown. Determined. Maybe a little sad? No, sad didn't quite fit. Lonely?

Like Claire used to tell him directly, and Dr. Washingtonn a tad less directly, he was not great at identifying or dealing with feelings, especially his own. So when that outrage exploded in this woman's eyes—yes, outrage, he pinned that one—his mind just went blank.

Part of him knew he should have stuck around to help her with the mess, of course he should. But the rest of him? With all that dangerously crackling energy directed his way? *Screw that*, was his instant thought. And the rest of him threw up its hands and surrendered to the familiar urge to run.

Fortunately, his gig at the hospital was a perfectly legitimate excuse for not hanging around to help Angry-at-Him Lady. Dr. Washingtonn and Claire might call him out on that statement, but they were not here, were they?

Besides, from what he could tell, the stuff in that woman's boxes, the stuff that had crumbled to a fine silt under his boot, it was only Christmas cookies. Fancy Christmas cookies, something told him, probably for a bunch of snobs. He pictured the cutesy, pastel cartons she was holding on her arms, they had oval emblems on them, *Amy's Bakery,* or something like that.

Not Amy. He thought for a second. No, the script had read, *Anna.*

Anna's Bakery.

So yeah, cookies. Or cupcakes. Or fussy pastries.

No big deal.

No big deal. The phrase that had ended his marriage. The words he had come to say too often after losing Noah because, *whatever*; nothing had mattered much anymore.

He used the phrase less these days, mainly because he talked to other humans less these days.

But also because even if he couldn't force himself to care about, for example, a few boxes full of designer cookies for very rich people, it didn't mean they weren't important to someone else. Someone else like, for example, Angry-Lady, maybe lonely, pretty-eyed Anna.

He rephrased. Not *no big deal.* But also not the end of the world. He, on the other hand, had ill kids and worried-sick parents to try to entertain. If anyone should be angry, shouldn't it be him?

Okay, maybe not. Even he got that, but still.

He checked the map on his phone again, less than a quarter-mile to go. That alley had been a mistake; instead of saving him time, the supposed shortcut and collision with Anna only ended up costing him some.

At the next three intersections, he crossed before the sign signaled it was his turn. As he hurried, he supported the underside of the belly like some pregnant women did, including Claire a lifetime ago. Waving urgently and apologetically with his free hand at each crosswalk, he jogged past the lanes of slowing cars and honking drivers, and *finally!* He let out a long breath as he entered the hospital's sliding glass doors.

* * *

He stopped short and stood still. Squared his shoulders, took a deep breath. *Only two hours. You can do this.*

Slowly he looked around, got his bearings and, whoa, this...this was truly impressive. The lobby atrium had been completely overhauled into a giant wintry North Pole, beachy California-themed Christmas amusement park mashup—a fantastic one.

As he looked around the room, he recognized the small-scale Orange County icons: the Huntington Beach Pier, a twinkling Queen Mary ship replica, floating on a sea of mirrors beside a kid-sized ice-skating rink, the Irvine Christmas Train. The snaking tracks circled the entire lobby and led to a picket-fenced area with a street sign that read, *North Pole.* Inside the gate sat a giant sleigh with eight reindeer on a ramp that made it look like the whole thing was about to take flight. The sleigh was heaped with wrapped gifts and, beside it, was Santa's big ol' red-velvet and gold-trimmed chair.

Totally over the top but even he—gloomy as he had been the last few years—had to admit, pretty freakin' amazing.

James' memory of the decorations the December Noah was here was thick with dark clouds, and although hazy, simply trying to recall tugged him back in time. He and Claire, that Christmas, they were so heartbroken and zombie-level exhausted. Santa had visited Noah in his room. Probably James hadn't come down to the party. Who knew?

Today, he let himself pause and take it in, although only for a moment—something inside him still felt guilty for appreciating holiday cheer. Like he was sneaking the forbidden. Frivolous and unnecessary. Like the fun and joy of the holiday wasn't meant for him; rather, like some imaginary restaurant happy-table that had a big fat *Reserved* sign plopped down on it, saved for someone else.

Snap out of it, sad sack. Right *now*.

Over there, by the scaled-down locomotive that was decked out in colorful lights, he spotted his PR contact, Jo, wearing a dark-green dress. With a deliberate smile on his face, he headed toward her.

"Santa! I mean, James," she said, bringing a hand to her mouth. "I'm so glad you're here; I was starting to worry. We're still waiting for a few more key people to arrive"—she looked at her watch nervously—"But you're here." She opened her arms to give him a collegial hug. "Thank you again for agreeing to do this on your day off—we're thrilled. The kids and parents are just starting to come down."

Jo hooked him up with a lavalier mic, and he stuffed the transmitter in his red coat's inside pocket. Nearby, elevator doors opened, and the first arrivals emerged: kids, staff, and parents with stuffed toys, wheelchairs, and IV poles. Their eyes popped when they saw the lobby, and smiles... delighted smiles appeared on nearly every single face.

One young boy caught James' eye as he yanked on his mother's arm and excitedly pointed toward him, at Santa. The boy's reaction, James reminded himself, was why he had pushed himself to do this, and he waved a small *hello* across the room, hand close by his side, just for this one little child.

But he could not focus on only one kid; he had a big job to do.

Own it, man.

Patting his belly and standing tall, "Ho, ho, ho," he called, projecting his voice as he waved and began to circle the large room. He moved slowly, doing his best imitation of a Santa-befitting saunter. Kids laughed, parents eyed one another with relief at what James knew might be an uncommon moment of gladness.

Seeing the kids as he walked around and *ho-ho-ho*'ed, damn it but he couldn't control it—this is just what he was afraid of—a lump of sadness began to form in his throat.

Compartmentalize, push the melancholy away, that was the thing to do. And he was free to do it now without feeling guilty or letting anyone down. Claire was not around to call him a robot with no feelings. But anyway, she had been so wrong; it wasn't that he didn't feel anything back then, or now, it was that those feelings—the immense worry, the crushing grief, the anger at what seemed like so much unfairness—they held him underwater; they completely overwhelmed.

That same little guy caught James' eye again, and this time he wore an expectant look.

Pressure. James picked up on the boy's anticipation. It snapped him out of the momentary gloom and back into his proper role—today he wasn't the reclusive hospital chef or the still-grieving father; no, he was Santa freaking Claus.

"Hey, everybody!" he boomed into his mic, drawing their attention. "So. I have a question." He scrunched his face and rubbed the Santa beard by his mouth, pretending to be confused. "Um, what holiday is it?" he asked the crowd that was forming a circle around him.

Nervous laughter, but no answer.

"Wait, don't tell me. I know. Yes! It's the fourth of July."

Genuine laughter now, and this time the kids screamed in unison, "No!"

"Okay, hmmm, I see. Wait, we're all dressed up." He pointed to the elves by the sleigh, and then looked down, surprised, at himself. "With these costumes, then it must be... I know. Is it Halloween?"

"No!" they yelled again, and even a few skeptical teenagers standing off to the side joined in.

"No?" He made a pouty face and rubbed the beard again, looked down in exaggerated bewilderment at his Santa suit. "Maybe *you* should all tell *me*." He pointed to the crowd and then back at himself. "Okay now, let me know: *What* day is it?" Quickly, he brought his hand to his ear.

James' smile reached his eyeballs with zero effort as the sound of the kids' voices hit his ears. "Christmas Eve!"

He made a puzzled face and put his palm by his ear again. "What? I can't hear you."

"It's Christmas Eve," the kids screamed even louder. And then without him prompting, they repeated, "Christ*mas*!"

The voices, so many little voices, what a wonderful sound.

"Okay, well..." He shrugged, raised his eyebrows, pretended to act surprised. "In that case, I guess we're in luck. Old St. Nick is here, and *now*"—he pumped his fist in the air as the DJ at the edge of the ice-skating rink spun the first notes of a "Jingle Bells" pop-rock remake. "*Now* the party can get started."

Chapter 3
rerouting...

Breathe. Anna set the three remaining boxes down on the metal counter in the back room to take stock.

Damn it to hell. She could kick herself—and that guy—why had she tried to carry more? The boxes were dented where she must have tightened her grip, and her body tensed as she lifted each lid to assess. There were a lot of crumbs but by some Christmas miracle a few layers of cookies remained intact.

Okay, come up with a plan. Prioritize.

The hospital's lunchtime party had already started, and soon the kids and their parents would be looking for dessert. From these boxes and the ones she had safely loaded in the van earlier, she could just about salvage the hospital's portion. Anna looked at what was here: the boat parade sailboats for her one most picky client and the Rudolphs in the sports cars. They weren't the cookies she had planned for the kids, but Jo had told her the theme was SoCal winter wonderland. These weren't ideal, but they would still fit the theme.

There, part one of the contingency plan, decided.

Then, instead of staying at the party as planned, she could hurry back here after the drop-off and re-bake the rest of the orders. She would call each client and explain. With any luck she would only be a couple of hours late.

Okay, not so bad. She could fix this. It was, actually, probably—yes, it was definitely—doable.

But... *No*.

A sick feeling washed over her, and she spun around to the mixing area, slid back the lid on the storage container under the counter. A few tablespoons of white crystals framed the bottom of the sugar bin like snowflakes in a windowpane corner.

The bakery was supposed to get a big delivery yesterday, but her distributor called and told her a Midwest snowstorm would delay it a couple of days. She had enough on hand to bake her Christmas orders, but the shop had been so busy she forgot to run to the restaurant supply store for her usual backup, just-in-case reserve.

That would be the same store that was now closed, like every other store within a reasonable driving radius.

Not once in four years had she missed a delivery. Sure, there were mix-ups on occasion. Like the time an employee had put a bachelorette's erect, extra-large penis cookies into a box destined for a ninetieth birthday party. Anna never found out if it was a practical joke or honest mistake, but it didn't matter. Errors were rare and luckily that customer's family had a sense of humor, plus Anna always apologized profusely and made amends. But today was Christmas Eve, and these were her top clients. The ones she bent over backward for, the ones whose orders she hand-delivered, the ones she did *not* let down.

The ones she could not afford to lose.

She would have to do major damage control to make up for this—deliver a bottle of top-shelf champagne, give them all a year's worth of free cookies. *If* they came back to her. For the most part her clients were nice people, but they also had incredibly high expectations. After the New Year, she would talk to the bank about a loan to cover the potential shortfall in meeting operating expenses.

That arrogant, sauntering Santa guy. Now it was not just *late* cookies but absolutely *no* cookies at all. But she had to stick to her plan, or she would also let down the kids at the hospital. Then as soon as she was done delivering, she would call her clients and grovel and explain, let them know about the debacle.

While carefully, very carefully, she moved the remaining cookies into new boxes, she mentally ran through the list of waiting customers and role-played the calls she would need to make. Thinking about the bad news she so hated to break made her feel incompetent, not in control, and the worst of all: vulnerable.

One name in particular made her heart lurch and sink: Guy, the managing partner of the Angels, her potential investors. Her fist clenched and she banged it on the counter. Thank you very much, Santa Claus. On top of bailing on her top customers, her dream of a second location —her larger space with the marble island so she could grow her business—now that would also be at stake.

Since the day she had gotten that invitation to the Angels' biggest event, sometimes early in the mornings when it was quiet here or at home at night once Carli was asleep, she would allow herself to picture it in full, realistic detail, Anna's Bakery of Cookies number two. Not because she wanted some kind of empire to her name or a lot of money. No, she was not like that. What it meant to her was protection, of her heart and livelihood, both. It meant safety from others' rash decisions, and security for the kids. It meant keeping a connection to her mother and the baking they did together when Anna was young, and even when she was a grown adult.

And the secret hope she had not and would not share aloud: that she could create something that Carli or Ben could take over one day if they chose, something that would give them the protection and security Anna so prized.

But right now, priorities and first thing first: The children at the hospital, she would not let those kids down today, so finish reshuffling the uninjured cookies and drop them off at the party, stat.

* * *

The children's hospital atrium had transformed into a sparkling Christmas fantasyland, just like Jo, the new PR director, had said. The organizers and hospital leadership clearly spared no expense. Huge twirling ornaments hung from the glass dome ten stories high. On the ground, famous landmarks filled the entire lobby. A tunnel, dark but strung with holiday lights in the shapes of a floating boat parade; a jungle gym in a Huntington Pier motif, The Queen Mary, next to an ice rink large enough for actual skating, a replica of the Irvine Christmas Train.

Anna turned so she could look all the way around. Many of the attractions were places she had visited with Carli and Ben when they were younger. A thought flashed of Carli and the stupid watch, and Anna wished she could be here to see this. Maybe it would get her to feel a shred of appreciation. She and Ben were healthy, and they had gotten to visit these actual spots, not a hospital lobby simulation.

What a stellar display, even more elaborate than last year. Evergreen trees in the corner set off the North Pole area, including a giant sleigh piled with presents. In front of it, at varying heights, eight reindeer rose, staged as if galloping up and into the air. Nearby was Santa's big throne, red and gold and raised on a dais. The platform looked like a wooden boardwalk that reminded her of the San Clemente Pier. Seeing it gave her an idea—a new cookie design for next year.

Through the fake trees and over a cute white picket fence, she could see a brigade of elves escorting kids to... obviously it must be Santa, standing near the sleigh. It was hard to see from way over here, with the long, winding line and so much barely controlled chaotic activity. The train whistle howled; the DJ played carols; elves danced with the patients in queue, and with their moms and dads.

Jo spotted Anna and hurried toward her to say hello. She wore a gorgeous jade-green cocktail dress. Anna felt her cheeks heat at the thought of the two holiday dresses still hanging behind the door in her office, the festive wrap-dress she had planned to wear here to the party and the floor-length ball gown she had gotten for the gala later. But the cookie fiasco had stolen, among other things, her time to change.

She smoothed her white baker's coat self-consciously as Jo led her to a long, decorated buffet table, safely set off from the hustle and bustle in the area in back of Santa's throne. While the two of them chatted, Anna quickly unpacked the cookies and arranged them on the etageres she dropped off last week. When she happened to glance up between boxes, an adorable little girl in the distance was chatting away merrily with Santa. From behind, this gentleman seemed animated and upbeat, nothing like the distracted grouch who ran off after crashing into her and knocking her cookies to the ground.

Anna shouldn't be thinking this, since men simply were not part of her life anymore, but blame it on that sexy dream: This Santa's build, his demeanor and focus on the kids, his body language from this vantage point, she could not help it: She wanted to watch him.

But parents and kids wandered over to check out dessert. They oohed and aahed at the boats with the golden icing and the race cars with the crazed fondant reindeer drivers. Between watching Santa and seeing the children's reactions when they eagerly dug into the cookies, Anna's heart warmed, then melted. She had made the right decision. It was worth the consequences to help bring these kids the minutest bit of holiday cheer, to have made them some special Christmas treats.

She thought of her mother, who started their baking tradition the first Christmas after her father left. Her mother would be happy, thrilled, to know that, although in a different way, Anna was carrying on her hospital-volunteering tradition.

And just like that, everything angry began to fall away: Carli's complaining, Blake, his chic and perky wife, even the other Santa, that moron on the street. Okay, maybe not *everything* angry. Because *that* Santa, he really frosted her buns, and no, she was not willing to let go of that so fast.

Jo thanked her for supplying the cookies again, and Anna explained that unfortunately this year she would not be able to stay for the rest of the party. Jo smiled warmly, placed her hand on Anna's arm. "I understand, and you've done such a wonderful thing today for the kids. If you can spare just a few more minutes, we'd love to get photos of you with the other donors and volunteers."

"Of course, I'd love to," Anna replied, glancing down at her outfit again. It was not a holiday dress, but her chef's coat with embroidered logo was passable given her role; it was professional for a baker, and thankfully free of icing smudges and food coloring. Her smart flared black pants also were okay; they were a heavily discounted end-of-season designer splurge. And at least she had remembered to swap her clunky old backroom clogs at the bakery's rear door for her favorite black patent-leather ballet flats.

"Fabulous," Jo said, waving her hand, "Let's introduce you to Santa."

"Hold on one second." Anna took one of the reindeer cookies and swaddled it in a napkin. "He's got quite the job, let me bring him a snack."

Jo chatted about the decorations as they walked across the North Pole to the sleigh and the elves, and to Santa, who still wasn't seated but standing beside his throne. Two teens who had just been talking with him moved on to the sleigh to pick out a gift, and Jo put her hand on Santa's shoulder. As soon as he turned around, Anna sucked in a sharp breath—

You!

That full head of fake white hair, the same fake gold spectacles, the bushy eyebrows that would make it hard to see.

No, it can't be.

But it could be because, here he was. It was his eyes that gave him away, familiar blue eyes that stared back at her in disbelief, wide as saucers.

Chapter 4

you

When James happened to glance up between kids, Jo was coming toward him with another woman, and she made him look twice. The one in the white jacket, she struck him as vaguely familiar, and she carried something small in a napkin.

Small, like cookies.

Right. The universe had a sadistic sense of humor. It was her, Very-angry-at-him-Anna-the-baker-lady.

At seeing her again, a strange sensation stirred in his torso that wasn't caused by an injury from their crash or from the weight of the silicone belly. No, it stirred like some tingly thing. Some tingly, spice blend—a dry, heady mix of surprise, recognition, and a rare ingredient he could not identify.

Until reality snapped him right back like a thick rubber band. She was probably about to resume her verbal barrage. *Why didn't he watch where he was going? What kind of idiot runs around* outside *in a Santa costume?*

Hi, yeah, that idiot would be me.

That self-protective instinct to gird against someone

else's anger welled up; he was about to get hit with more wrath. But these were just cookies, he reminded himself trying to silence the little voice in his head that warned, *This party might feel like a loooong two hours.*

His pulse quickened as Jo introduced them, joking that of course his real name wasn't actually Santa.

"No, I'm afraid it's not, and now the truth is out." He hoped humor would defuse the situation as he extended his hand toward her. "Anna, I presume?"

"Oh, you two know each other!" Jo clasped her hands in delight, while Anna stood there looking...not only furious but also now flustered.

"We've, um, run into each other before," he said, and his teeth grit sheepishly. "It's nice to see you again," he added.

Maybe he shouldn't have cracked a smartass type of joke; the look on her face told him it might have been inappropriate. And just then Jo's phone rang and with a raised index finger she indicated she would need a moment.

Just great. She walked away, leaving him alone with Anna.

A lovely Anna, he had to say now that they were standing so close.

Despite that look she was giving him.

Being face to face, he wanted another chance to explain. On the street, there had been no real opportunity, just his shouted apologies as he rushed off. "I'm so sorry about what happened earlier; it must have been a huge inconvenience. Like I said, some sand or something blew into my eye and for a few seconds I really couldn't see where I was going." Story of his life. "I'm sorry I didn't stay to help you."

Smoke didn't billow out her ears, and her soft lips and pretty eyes softened, or at least that's what he wanted to see. After all, now that he realized she also must have been on her way here—with cookies for the kids—he had basically ruined what must have been a carefully laid out day.

Not to mention all the fancy cookies he busted up.

She stood watching him as if she didn't know what to say. The feeling in his chest grew warm and, at the realization she hadn't started to rip him a new one, it expanded. Her lips and intense eyes, he could see now they might actually be capable of a dash of kindness.

Maybe it was the relief that possessed him to continue, to shut off the filter he should permanently affix to his mouth, to say stuff before it was time. "...and you seemed really, like, steaming furious, and..."

Ramble much?

And still, despite his self-observation, heaven only knows why, he went on. "I... I know this is going to sound terrible. I'm sorry again, but I didn't have time to wait for you to calm down."

The eyes that held a hint of kindness a second ago narrowed and her soft, pretty lips did a kind of a pursing thing.

"But it turned out okay, right?" He kept barreling ahead. "I mean, catastrophe averted because, well, here you are." He gestured toward the table where kids were excitedly pointing and grabbing the cookies and grinning like fools when they took bites. "Look at them. They're totally thrilled. Besides,"—he did have the presence of mind to hold back the *no big deal*—"it's only cookies. The kids don't care if a few broke or some icing got smudged."

* * *

A lot was going on in Anna's mind, and in spite of those thoughts, also elsewhere in her body. At first he actually seemed kind of cute. The delighted kids, the incredible decorations, they made her not want to hold a grudge. When he first started to speak, he seemed sweet and earnest. And, she hated to admit it, but behind the Santa disguise he was very good looking, even...*sexy*? But wait, here it was. Why had she let herself even for a moment expect anything different? He was all but outright saying that his leaving her with the mess was her fault because she had been the angry woman, the bitter, demanding one.

So while he might have a fantastic build and sincerity in his eyes, her anger flared back at what he just said. How dare he insinuate that his abandonment was *her* fault?

She again resumed the fantasy she had nursed in the car. How she might—without causing serious, irreparable harm (it was Christmas Eve after all)—like to maim him.

A swift kick to the jingle balls.

A finger-jab to the base of the throat.

Or, something—she couldn't recall the precise name of the move, but it had to do with the Adam's apple.

"*Only* cookies?" she managed to sputter. "It might seem like only cookies to you, but for me and my family, it's my livelihood, and for my customers whose orders were smashed on the ground, they're hardly nothing."

He muttered and squeaked and nodded, as if he suddenly heard how clueless and diminishing his comment must have come across. "No, no. What I meant..."

She wasn't going to wait to hear more excuses. "James," she said sharply, "Do you have kids?"

His head pitched forward ever so slightly and he blinked a couple of times, winced like something invisible just stung him before giving her an odd look. "No," he said under his breath and pressed his lips together.

"Well, I do. And they require occasional feeding, shelter, and a few articles of clothing, which is expensive in southern California. And...college tuition. So it's not *just"*— she did the air quotes thing to emphasize her point— *"cookies* to me." Then she slid her hand into her jacket pocket and felt the comfort of her phone; she would search the internet for that Adam's apple move and find instructions so she could learn it pronto.

His lips slowly unknotted, although now he looked weary. "I would have been furious in your shoes too," he said, "I really would be, Anna. I didn't mean that the cookies weren't important. It's your business, and also, look how happy you've made everybody with them today." He pointed again at the tables where the kids were eating. "But in that split second, I had a choice to make—help you or get here to play Santa for the kids. I'm sorry," he said, sounding utterly defeated. "But I picked the patients and their party."

His words were like a flat palm to her chest, stopping her from plowing ahead. Maybe she would hold off on the web search—at least for a couple of hours. Because what he said, the way that voice of his uttered her name, the solemn look on his face that told her he was taking it seriously, those things all conspired to change her perspective.

"I haven't lived here that long, and I took a wrong turn— several wrong turns in fact. That's why I was in the alley; that's why I was using my phone. And then that damn gust of wind blew, like I already said, it blew something in my face. Anyway. I'm repeating myself but I really am sorry— clearly, I didn't see you until it was too late."

Now she should say something, but watching him speak, well, it had become distracting. His blue eyes were compassionate—at this close distance, she could not convince herself otherwise. And that gentle smile of his, it perfectly matched their twinkle. Wait, twinkle wasn't the right word. It wasn't a sparkly, cliché love-story kind of eye twinkle but more like a glimmer, a pinpoint of steady light. An alert presence. A mature and wise twinkle. Eyes that said, "I'm here." Eyes that maybe even signaled—despite how recent events appeared—constancy. And grit, also seriousness, and yes, now she could see it, a note of sadness.

Damn it. There simply was no way to stay so furious at those eyes any longer. "I understand," she told him, surprising herself. "Apology accepted." And then, she decided to meet him halfway. "I broke my own rule against carrying too many boxes, and I should have been paying more attention. If I had, maybe I could have...avoided you."

He didn't say anything, just kept flashing her his damn tranquil yet arousing smile. His shoulders rose; his chest—his very broad chest—expanded. He inhaled a relieved breath, and she found herself glad to see him relax.

Around them, the photographer was still corralling the group for the pictures—elves in front, board members behind them, Jo and her PR staff flanking Santa. "Actually, Anna, you should be next to him," she said, "Why don't you both take a seat in his chair?"

James' mouth formed a pleased, if victorious, smile, and she had to admit it didn't annoy her; now that she knew him just a little more, it didn't strike her as smug.

Although she did not really know him.

That feeling of...well, of what whatever that feeling was, it did not mean she knew him. Heck, she had known Blake most of her adult life and she had not really known him. *Had* she?

No.

James climbed the three steps to the velvet throne and slid to one side while Anna stepped up and sat down beside him, resting her elbow on the swirly armrest. While the photographer adjusted elf hats down in the front row, James turned to her. His gaze on her face, it made something flutter and tingle low in her body, a place that had not felt fluttery or tingly in a long, long while.

This was totally absurd and completely out of left field but briefly she wondered if, the way his eyes slowly moved around her face, his focus, and that tingly, fluttery way she felt, he was about to ask if he could kiss her.

Totally absurd.

"May I?" he asked in a slow, hushed voice, his hands moving toward her temples as if he were about to lift a wedding veil.

Right. Her hairnet.

Her cheeks again grew hot. "Please. When I left the shop..." she made an embarrassed sigh. "I can't believe I forgot."

His fingers brushed her skin, and instinctively she shut her eyes to enjoy his light caress.

"You were busy cleaning up crumbs and rescuing cookies for the children's hospital." His breath tickled the top of her ear.

"True."

"But I have to say, it's giving you this cool lunch-lady vibe."

That drew a laugh from deep in her belly and in that moment, she realized, it wasn't only sex of which she had been deprived.

James laughed also, and my oh my, that simple act changed his countenance.

"Maybe you should leave it on," he said, his eyes getting involved in the discussion.

She slapped the back of his hand playfully. "Hurry, please. Take it off."

The words echoed in her mind.

Don't go there.

Carefully he removed it, and then the two bobby pins, watched intently as her hair fell and brushed her shoulders. Up close, she noticed the long fingers of his big strong hands.

"There you go," he said softly, handing the net and the two pins to her to stick in her pocket. From beside him, she could see that strange protrusion rise and fall underneath his beard when he spoke. It was actually...when you saw it in the context of the rest of his face—the parted lips, the aquiline nose, that steadfastness in his eyes that made him seem solid and reliable—yes, that bulge could be construed as alluring.

It must have been that dream last night, because it was hard to remember the last time she had paid so much attention to a man's appearance—and not just looks but his being, his presence. Between work and the kids and Blake's never-ending annoyances, her days were over-full; at night she was usually so tired, she fell sound asleep before she could let her mind wander to anything else.

The photographer snapped away. Serious photos with the hospital CEO, silly photos of the elves, several shots of Santa and Anna hamming it up to post on everyone's social feeds. By the time the session finished, the tension in her shoulders had loosened. James stepped down from the chair first, then took Anna's hand to help her, and they left the North Pole together.

But this unusual sense of ease was short-lived as the truth of the situation crept back into her consciousness. Inconspicuously, she glanced at the clock above the elevator bank and a twin sense of dread and shame rose in her gut. Like Cinderella at the ball, her time was running out. She could put it off no longer; she had to call the customers and finally tell them. Unfortunately, she was going to be the one to ruin their expectant holiday night.

* * *

Jo caught up with them just as they were through the picket gate on the way to the tables with what remained of Anna's cookies. "James," Jo said, "the charge nurse just texted about a few kids upstairs, immunocompromised so it's dangerous for them to come down. The DJ's about to take a break, and the a cappella chorus is going to start singing in a few minutes. Once the concert starts, would you be willing to make a visit to their rooms? I have to stay down here but I trust you can find your way around?"

She handed him a high-quality mask, sealed in clear plastic from her pocket, and he took it and said okay. But his face... Anna grew concerned. He looked as if he suddenly felt sick.

Jo must have noticed it too, because she explained: "We had a doctor who was going to play Santa upstairs, but a patient needed an urgent procedure and he was called away."

"It's fine, no problem," he said, although the set of his mouth said otherwise while he stared at the package with the mask. Clearly the request unnerved him. And although Anna couldn't articulate exactly why, the words flew out of her mouth without a fraction of a second's thought. "James, I can go with you."

The way he looked at her, it made her forget temporarily about her clients; in fact, it almost made her cry.

"That's alright; it's something I need to do as Santa, but

it's nice of you to offer." Jo's phone rang again, and she answered and told the caller, "Yes, yes, of course, I'll be right there." She ended the call, thanked James and Anna both, pointed toward the west side of the atrium. "Duty calls. The ice-skating rink is starting to melt."

As soon as they were alone, Anna asked him again because his expression still looked pained. "Really, it's fine," he said, "I'll go alone."

She was unsure what to say next, but it didn't matter. "While we were taking the photos," he went on, "I thought more about what happened earlier and how the kids couldn't care less about the cookies' condition but, tell me the truth, how bad was all of the damage?"

They approached the table with the food, with nothing but crumbs left on the cookie etageres. She hesitated, wavering between honesty and, surprisingly, not wanting him to feel worse. "It wasn't great, but"—she gestured to the nearly empty trays—"like you said, here I am." She shrugged. "At least I was able to salvage enough for the kids."

"But...did you have other customers?" he asked, stopping to look at her, taking ahold of her shoulder.

She nodded yes, because something about his here-ness, his presence, made her tell the painful, pathetic truth.

"Oh, no," he exclaimed and then immediately asked, "What are you going to do?"

A sigh escaped. "There's nothing I *can* do. I ran out of ingredients, and by the time I realized it, the stores were closed."

It hurt physically, although it was actually her pride, to say those words aloud. From day one, she had dotted every I and crossed every T. For every possible scenario, she had a policy, a rule, a backup plan—if not two.

And yet. A simple mishap and she had left herself with no solution.

"What are you missing?" His contracted brow showed real concern, and when he took his hand off her shoulder, she felt instantly lonely, less reinforced, without it.

"This is so embarrassing." She brought her palms to her eyes and closed them. "I hate to even say it; I'm usually über-careful and proactive."

"It can't be as embarrassing as not looking where you're going and crashing into the baker who has her arms full of special cookies to deliver on Christmas Eve. Tell me, Anna," he lowered his deep voice until its consistency was smooth and velvety, just above a whisper. "Tell me," he coaxed, "What is it you need?"

Not fair. He should not use her name like that, or that tone, all reassuring and intimate. It set off more of that strange, fluttery sensation all the way down to her toes, sensation that after so long she wasn't sure whether she wanted more of, or she hated.

"Sugar. Sugar for sure. And maybe also...butter. I didn't have time to check." She cringed. Two of the most basic ingredients.

Sheesh, Anna, are you sure you have flour? Come to think of it, do you even know how to bake?

The smile that spread across his face, it dislodged the thick mustache from the corner of his mouth. His bushy fake eyebrows wiggled, and the real skin at the corner of his eyes pinched into an enthusiastic accordion crinkle. "Quick detour before I go upstairs. Follow me," he said all confident and commanding as he waved his arm. "I'm about to make you a very happy lady."

Chapter 5
one condition

As soon as James said it, he pictured plenty more he might be able to do to make her a happy lady in addition to giving her what he was planning. But why was he thinking about that? He was in no shape or position to connect with someone else, to share any feelings whatsoever. Anna might be lovely and compassionate, easy on the eyes and unassuming, but he was not ready to travel Relationship Road again, no siree, not even for a hookup.

Just, no.

As they walked down the corridor, lights flicked on from their motion, and his phone vibrated from the pocket inside his Santa coat. Without breaking their stride, he pulled it out to silence it. Only two people were likely to be calling him, and they would either be the headhunter or Claire. One of them he was in no rush to speak to; the other he could call back later.

When they got to the door, he pulled his lanyard and badge out from the coat's other interior pocket. He swiped the plastic through the reader and the *Food Service* door clicked open.

"You work here, at the hospital?" she asked, standing in the doorway behind him.

"I do."

"Wait a second. Are you the new chef?"

He was leading her toward the shelves of dry goods, but at her question he paused to turn and answer. "Guilty as charged."

"Wow, okay. I read about you in the newspaper. You're originally from Orange County, moved away, opened a restaurant, and returned a few months ago, right?

"In a nutshell, yes." *And outside the nutshell, went bankrupt at the same time the rest of my life imploded.* "I came back for the job," he replied, pointing to a lone ten-pound bag of sugar on the middle shelf. "We only have one. Our shipment's"—she finished the sentence with him, an I-know-where-this-is-going tone to her silky voice—"been delayed."

He took the bag off the shelf, and she reached out to take it from him, but instead of handing it over, he held it close to his chest. "You can have this under one condition."

"And what is that?" she asked, biting her cheek like she was trying to tamp her grin.

"Tell me, what did you do with the busted-up cookies, I mean the ones that didn't fall out of the boxes and onto the ground?"

"They're on the counter at my shop."

"Then I'll make you a very special Christmas deal," he said.

"A deal?" Her eyes joined the grin, giving her face an open, relaxed look that felt like a gift to witness.

"The sugar is yours, and I'll throw in ten pounds of butter to be safe—it's all I have on hand and, by the way, it's not at room temperature. In exchange, you have to give me the broken cookies."

"Okay, but what are you going to do with them?"

"I have to prepare dessert for the kids tomorrow, and without the sugar I need something else to work with. Cookie crumbles will be equally sweet. Come to think of it, it's pretty renegade and counter-culture, the idea of imperfect, broken cookies. The kids will love them; they'll be a hit."

"Great idea. That's a deal I'm more than willing to make. Thank you." She tilted her head adorably and sighed a relieved sigh. "This is amazing."

"After what happened, giving you some sugar and butter is the least I can do."

And then the grin she was nibbling on narrowed into something more serious, but her open expression remained. "It was an accident, James."

She touched his forearm as she spoke. Technically, she touched the shaggy red material of his oversized sleeve, but it didn't matter; it still had the same warming effect in his closed-off, disconnected, cold-hearted chest. Maybe the deep freeze of his emotional life, actually of his whole life in general, was why her touch was so noticeable, so distinct.

So arresting.

"Don't keep beating yourself up," she was saying now. "If it's alright, I'll bring the broken cookies by first thing in the morning."

"That's good," he managed, suddenly nervous about seeing her again. "I'm here starting at six, and I just need them sometime before ten. I know that's early on Christmas Day, but"—he turned toward the shelf again although he'd already taken down the sugar, and he closed his eyes for a split second. As if that could give him a boost of nerve.

Grow a pair, dude. "I'll make you a good cup of coffee. Does that work with your schedule?"

"It does. Christmas is a rare day off, and good coffee would be an extra treat." She bobbed her head slightly left and right, awkwardly like she wasn't sure what came next. "So, um, I should get back to the shop and start baking."

"Go. Skedaddle. I'll stay out of your way, no more wind-blown skulking for me anywhere near your alley."

Skedaddle? Not that he was trying to get lucky but if he had any hope of it at any point in his future, he should update his vocabulary.

At least she chuckled, if only out of pity. "Good luck, Santa," she said, looking his costume up and down. "Since it's Christmas Eve, I'm assuming you're in for a long, busy night."

He patted the belly, leaned back on his heels. "It's a tough job. Or, actually more like picking up takeout tacos after the hospital party."

Why did he just say that? Now she would assume he had no life outside this hospital kitchen. Which, he didn't. But which didn't matter anyway because he was not trying to flirt or date or do anything like have sex.

"Let me guess: al pastor, with extra guacamole, from *Paloma's* food truck around the corner."

"Not bad. That would be a yes on the al pastor, but I don't like avocado. And I always get my tacos from *Achiote*, which is also nearby, fortunately down the block. They have the best tacos. With all due respect to Paloma."

"I don't think so," she said. "My kids and I have eaten a lot of tacos around here, and Paloma's truck is, hands down, the best."

Ah-ha! The disclosure of personal information. She was a mom. He could picture her holding the hands of two small kids as they ordered from the food truck and waited for their tacos.

No mention of a man. Note to self: Best practice to check on marital status *before* thinking about making Anna or anyone else a happy lady.

But then there went his mouth again without his brain's consent. "We might have to agree to disagree on that. Or, better yet, sometime let's do a taste test."

Whoa-ho, slow your roll, Santa man.

He didn't wait for her to politely decline whatever it was he just put out there. "How about you?" he asked rapid-fire. "What Christmas Eve plans do you have after you re-make all the cookies?"

Despite what she had just said, he pictured her with a man—a boyfriend, a partner, who she would bring to some fancy event at a friend's or client's house. She would wear a classy, sexy dress and sparkly makeup, high-heels and—he felt something stir to life below his belly—black stockings. For a split second he let himself imagine how fun it could be to take her to a Christmas party, and what he would like to do with her after, but quickly forced himself to snap out of it.

Not even a hookup.

"Once the orders are delivered, I have a... a thing, an event to attend. But it should end by ten, and after that my big plans are to make popcorn and, if I can stay awake any longer, I might watch a movie."

I, not we.

Her answer didn't necessarily confirm that she was single, although he got the strong feeling she was, and she wasn't wearing a ring.

But he reminded himself yet again, it didn't matter. He only had to think of the unpacked boxes in his apartment, of the many short stints on his résumé, of the call from Claire that would happen today or tomorrow and that always dragged his mood back into the past.

"Sounds fun," he said, now imagining her no longer in a sexy dress but in sweats, with her hair casual, messed up. Then, fortunately because he didn't know what else to say, she pointed toward the door and said she really should be going.

But before she left, she reached out and patted his big belly—not his actual belly but the padding. "James, if I could offer a few words of advice," she said, "be careful with this thing."

They both laughed at that, a laugh from deep inside, and it only lasted a couple of seconds but man, did it feel good. He liked watching how her eyes lit, but then he looked away. No point in getting hooked.

She slid the sugar and butter off the counter onto her forearms, then into an embrace—sugar on her left, butter on her right. He noticed from her movements that, like him, she was a southpaw.

Just as she turned to leave, she looked up and met his eyes once more. She really was lovely. Maybe he should follow up on that taco tasting thing so he could see her again after tomorrow's brief cookie-crumble drop-off, purely-platonic cup of coffee.

No, he told himself emphatically, and he pressed his lips tight while she said goodbye.

"I can't thank you enough, James. At first you did ruin my day but then you miraculously saved it."

* * *

The five o-clock stubble along his jawline where his beard didn't cover, the lips he nervously licked, the mussed salt and pepper hair Anna could barely make out under his wig —when he offered to make her a deal, all she could think was, *Yes. With very, very few exceptions, whatever it is, I'm in.*

Although what those exceptions might be, she was coming up short.

He had blurted out that taco tasting idea but then quickly deflected; maybe he realized it could sound like he might be asking her out. Only he wasn't, and she wouldn't have accepted anyway, even if he had been.

And now, she had more cookies to think about. They said goodbye, and she was on her way out, down the long, quiet corridor back to the hospital's atrium. Funny, she thought as she walked down the unfamiliar wing, that he was the new chef. Although, not exactly new; she had seen that article about his arrival way back in June or July. And also funny that the man who destroyed so many of her cookies would, just like the real Santa, be able to give her everything she lacked.

Okay, maybe not everything. But considering the day, sugar and butter were a satisfying start.

But his reaction to Jo's request about going to the floors to visit the sickest kids niggled at her heart. It obviously upset him, and she had tried to piece together why as they stood and talked by the cafeteria storeroom. She guessed he must have been up there before—maybe he had a child who was in the hospital, but earlier he said he didn't have kids, so that wasn't it. The hospital had been around for as long as she knew; it was possible James had been a patient himself when he was younger and the memories still haunted. But they had just met each other, and it wasn't right to pry.

Anyway, the reason was less important than the pain she had seen in his eyes. She stopped short in the hallway, turned around, went back to the food service door, from which he was just coming out. He adjusted the mask and headed toward the bank of elevators. The sad curl of his shoulders told her she was right to return, that whatever was going on with him took precedence over even her top clients.

"James, please," she said as she approached and startled him, judging by how suddenly he looked up. "It's not an imposition. Let me go with you to visit the kids." And then she had an idea: "I'll find Jo and see if she can locate an extra elf costume somewhere, and I can play Santa's helper."

His eyes widened and then he briefly shut them. The mask obscured his mouth, but the way the white material shifted, it betrayed a reluctant smile. "Anna. That's a great idea, funny and so kind," he said slowly as if trying to find the right words, "but it's fine. And besides, you have a big deadline."

He pointed down the hall, the corners of his eyes and the mask shifting again as he spoke, faster this time. "Now, go. Scram." He pointed again. "Get out of here, or I'll... revoke...yes, I'll revoke that sugar and the butter in your hands. Go and bake those cookies."

* * *

She took Pacific Coast Highway back to the bakery to avoid the 405. The PCH route was slow-going and further, but given traffic the 405 would take longer. Case in point, after only a few minutes, she stopped at the Main Street intersection in Seal Beach so the antique fire truck carrying Santa could turn onto PCH.

With her phone safely in the hands-free mount, one by one she called the customers to say their cookies would be late. She cringed each time she selected a new number and waited for them to answer, but at least she didn't have to say, *I'm so sorry but you know that Christmas cookie order you're expecting? Well, it's cancelled.*

And while she was awash with gratitude, thank goodness for mobile phones that made it possible for her to talk live to nearly every one of her people. She explained and apologized and asked about their afternoon and evening plans. She would re-coordinate her drop-off schedule, deliver first to the clients who had earlier needs.

There were only a couple of them she hadn't been able to reach: the laid-back stay-at-home mom who had mentioned needing the cookies for guests on Christmas Day, so she would have no issue, and the other was Guy, the head of the Angels, who was perpetually busy and probably in a meeting.

She left an especially contrite voicemail for him because his son's party was starting mid-afternoon but still, making contact was important; she would try again as soon as the first batch of cookies was baking in the oven.

As she ended her last apologetic call, she turned left into the alley and parked the van by the bakery's back door. Before getting out, she used the map app to plot a logical drop-off route based on the customers' schedules and to avoid crisscrossing Orange County. Carli might be on to something, Anna now had to admit. Talking into a smart watch that used AI would be better at delivery logistics than trying to tap and drop pins like breadcrumbs using the map on her phone.

Luckily, she had dropped the last pin when the battery died from all the calls and delivery choreography. She stuck the phone in her purse and made a mental note to plug it in inside.

At the door, she unlocked the deadbolt and once inside turned on the back-room lights. She brought in the sugar and butter from the van and set them on the counter by the mixer, put her hair up and into the net from her pocket, fixed it tight with the bobby pins that James had carefully handed back to her.

Next, she retrieved the printout of orders from her desk, washed her hands, assembled all the ingredients. She cross-checked that she had every item for the recipe hanging from the shelf over the counter. She knew her recipes by heart from so many years of baking them, but still, it was good to re-confirm each ingredient and its precise amount yet one more time. She washed her hands again and then finally—she heaved a heavy breath—*finally!* It was time to start baking.

For the first batch of cookie dough, she creamed the butter and sugar in the mixer's bowl—just long enough to combine—then added the extracts, vanilla and almond both. She hummed her favorite carols while she began to beat in the eggs, one by one. Then into another metal bowl she added the dry ingredients: baking powder, salt, organic flour.

While slowly adding the contents into the mixer bowl, she involuntarily pictured the way James had smiled as he handed her his sugar, how his eyes held that steady, knowing sparkle even though she could tell something was making him sad.

But involuntarily was the thing. Even though a little something, a feeling, might be blossoming in her midsection, it didn't mean she had to indulge it. He was a man, a handsome one, with a pleasant—maybe leaning ever so slightly toward magnetic—and sincere demeanor, and he had given her sugar and butter because...not because he was interested in her but because he had single-handedly, utterly, royally, messed up her busiest day of the entire year, and he felt bad.

But even if, just for the sake of argument, that steady sparkle he possessed was somehow trained on her, it didn't mean anything. He probably wore a wedding band she hadn't noticed underneath his white Santa glove.

Anyway, she had sworn off dating because her plate was eternally full—growth plans for the business, a teenage Carli still at home, the wound from Blake's betrayal of their family unit that had yet to fully heal.

When all the dry mix was in the mixer bowl, she quickly went to plug in her dying phone. It made a satisfying chirp when she connected the power cable, and the sound rekindled her gratitude. That was something she always tried to impress upon the kids—how they shouldn't take things for granted. She thought of Carli and the damn Spiralo AI watch. *Yeah, so much for that.*

But here Anna was in her element, safely ensconced in the back room of her shop. Here, she could do what she was good at and loved and that, after several years of investing sweat equity to build up her clientele, finally provided her and Ben and Carli a nice lifestyle, independent of what their father provided.

Another deep breath, another thank you to the universe for how this day turned out. Disaster averted; she was fixing the problem. The customers she had spoken to were not furious. The kids were safe and miles away, so she didn't feel pressure to hurry home. Life really was okay.

No, it was much more than okay; in fact it was quite good.

Quite good and complete and not missing a single thing. Like companionship or laughter, romance, or intimacy with a human. *No.* While those things might be nice to have, they always came at a heavy price. So no, thank you very much, just no. She would put all the thoughts and strange bodily sensations James evoked out of her mind. She was independent and content, not in need of any of that.

Chapter 6
from the mouths of babes

James planned—he really had planned—to ask Anna if he could help her bake and decorate the replacement cookies when he was done playing Santa. She would have said no, he was ninety-nine-point-nine-nine percent sure. She was so focused and self-sufficient. And he knew from his experience cooking and baking at a commercial scale, she would have her own routine, her zone, her flow, and she wouldn't want anyone interfering.

He would have liked to watch her work.

But just like the taco tasting, it was not going to happen. Even though it touched him deeply the way she had turned around, concerned, sincerely wanting to help him with the kids. She had made a sacrifice, prioritized his needs over her clients. An offer of comfort, a generous one, especially with the long afternoon she faced baking and delivering the orders he wrecked.

The sensor by the metal stairwell door beeped when he swiped his badge. A little huffing and puffing from taking the steps up to floor eight instead of the elevator would help settle his anxiety. Physical activity and—he drew a heavy breath to bring some more air into his lungs as he made his way up—thinking of Anna. He pictured her relief when she saw the package of sugar, remembered her unguarded smile. His guess was that she didn't smile like that often, relieved or carefree, and the pleasure of getting to see it reactivated that weird unravely feeling in his chest.

But the distraction she afforded was coming to a halt. At the top of the stairs, he came face to face with that familiar metal door. Widening his shoulders, he took another deep breath, set aside his hesitance, and grasped the handle to open it up.

He made his way around the carts in the hall, and waved jolly-Santa-like to the staff and the parents. It had been long enough ago that, fortunately, he didn't recognize any of their faces. Many of the rooms were empty, but at the next doorway he peeked around, a young boy in a sweatsuit was sitting on the edge of a bed.

James took another breath and knocked on the door-frame, and the boy's face broke into a surprised smile the instant he turned to look.

James did a quick age assessment as he walked into the room. Definitely not a toddler; not so much of a little kid; old enough likely to know the truth about Santa; maybe ten or eleven?

"Hi there," James said. "As you can probably tell, I'm Santa—at least for today. My real name is usually James."

That brought out a chuckle and the boy simultaneously nodded. "I'm Austin for today. My real name is also usually Austin."

Now James was the one to laugh at the kid's quick humor. "Nice to meet you Austin," *but you shouldn't be here. No kid should have to be in the hospital at Christmas— or any time of year.* "So...uh, how are you doing?"

Instead of daydreaming about Anna's bright eyes and soft lips and beautiful smile, James should have used his time in the stairwell to figure out his older-kid Santa schtick.

Austin hesitated for a beat but then answered. "I'm okay. How are you?" He jutted his chin at James' costume. "How's the party going?"

"I'm good," James blatantly lied, feeling the weight of sadness. "It's fun playing Santa, and the party, it's going alright. Although it's mostly for little kids. For you, I think it might be kind of a drag," he lied again. He pictured the ride-on train and the skating rink and the amazing light display. Even he had been wowed by the elaborate decorations. Including the giant sleigh piled with gifts.

Gifts. *Shoot.* He should have brought some with him, enough for the kids up here. What kind of lousy Santa was he, to show up, on floor eight of all places, empty-handed?

He rubbed his forehead and dropped his head. "Austin, man, I have to say I'm sorry."

Austin tilted his head, curious. "For what?"

"Apparently I'm a..." *No cursing.* "Apparently, I'm not a great Santa. I forgot to bring my bag of presents. I'll run downstairs." He raised his finger. "Be right back."

Austin put out his arm, making a gesture to stop him. James noticed a nasty bruise inside his elbow, probably from too many IVs, but he controlled the urge to look away, to pretend it wasn't there.

"You can stay," Austin said. "Don't worry about the presents, at least not for me. I don't need anything anyway."

So many things crossed James' mind as he struggled with how to respond.

Austin, however, showed far more maturity as well as verbal acumen. "Actually, I do want something. But I guess it's more of a wish than a thing."

"And what's that, what's your wish?" James asked, glad he didn't have to say so much, although his relief was short-lived. Tangible things like presents were easy to provide; wishes...those got into tricky personal and emotional territory and, technically, they weren't a Santa thing.

Or were they?

"I'm not afraid of...you know, the end. But..." he made an expression as if trying to steel himself, bit his lower lip while his measured breath pushed out his young chest. It was bravery, James identified, and so much more fortitude than he himself had been capable of. "My family—obviously I know the whole Santa thing isn't real so you can't personally do it—but my wish is that they won't stay sad. I want them to have fun again."

There was no controlling the surge of water that rose up from the bottom of James' eyes. For a change he didn't try to hide his feelings. It wouldn't have been possible anyway; the tears pooling in his lower lids were immediate and plentiful, but also, he owed Austin the same directness this kid fearlessly possessed.

James nodded and pressed his lips as he wiped his eyes with his white gloves. "It's still hard for me to talk about as you can see but I've been there myself. I lost my son five years ago. So I know from experience it might take your family some time" *because they'll miss you so incredibly much* "but I'm confident they'll do their best."

Hopefully better than me.

"And you're right, Austin," James went on. "Santa being able to solve our problems is bullshit—sorry." Austin's smile sparked at the inappropriate word. "But if you would like me to, I'll talk to your parents and tell them about your wish and what you just so wisely said."

Austin looked somber but even more so, relieved that someone understood. He nodded his approval. "After."

James' eyes welled up again, and he noticed a sheen in Austin's too, and then the boy reached for his phone on the bedside cart. "Can you give me your number," he asked, "and I'll tell them to contact you?"

"Yes, please." James recited his number while Austin tapped it into his contacts, and then they shook hands and said goodbye. Remarkably for those few seconds James didn't cry.

At the doorway, he raised his hand to wave without turning around but then Austin called his name. He looked over his shoulder in response, and Austin was again smiling. "You're actually an excellent Santa. A little heavy, but excellent."

After Austin, he visited the other kids, then jogged downstairs, and swung by the quiet, out-of-the-way wing where Dr. Washingtonn had her office. A few minutes remained of his Santa break before the concert would end. After six months of avoiding that part of the hospital, he could see if she was free, poke his head into her office for a second to show her he had kept his promise—something he hadn't been sure until today he would be able to do.

When he got there, though, a two-sided cardboard sign on her door read, "in session," and the more permanent sign was engraved with someone else's name. This made him feel relieved and also disappointed. *Yes, score two.* He was on quite a roll today with this identifying feelings thing. He would ask Jo about Dr. Washingtonn later if she had a free moment, although she was a new hire and might not know her.

He recalled how that December five years ago, her office had become a refuge, how he would wander down there every so often. If she was not with someone else, she would wave him in and invite him to sit. Sometimes she would ask him how things were going, and other times, as if she could magically read that he didn't have a word to say, she would just let him be. One time he sat there for at least an hour without uttering a sound. He remembered it like yesterday; while she did her paperwork, he just sat there, staring blankly at the cute Christmas ornament she kept on her desk.

He hurried back to the atrium remembering her compassion and her gentle nature. When he got there, the a cappella chorus was just finishing its finale, a doo-wop carol medley. As the singers swayed and snapped near the ice rink, he climbed up onto the Santa platform and took his rightful seat on the big red velvet throne.

The elves ushered a few more children to get in line after the concert. Once James finished speaking with each of them and directing them to the gift sleigh, he stepped down from the platform and went to find Jo. Technically, the party wasn't over for another twenty minutes, but he had done good work for the kids and now he needed to say goodbye. He would ask her about Dr. Washingtonn next week at work or, if she was off for the holiday, then as soon as she got back.

His brief but meaningful chat with Austin diminished some of the weariness that dogged him and kept him from living his life so narrowly. Austin said he wanted his family to have fun again, and that f-word was open to so much interpretation. But James sitting in his empty, lonely apartment tonight, surrounded by cardboard boxes that screamed transience, could not possibly meet anybody's definition.

Even the tacos would not make it better.

He didn't expect someone who hadn't experienced the

same kind of loss to fully get it, but Anna had realized something was wrong earlier and also tried to help, so perhaps he shouldn't assume. She was compassionate and bright and gorgeous, and Jo had said she donated cookies to the kids—not once, but every year. He suddenly realized he had no idea what motivated her to bake for the patients, no idea about her reasons. So what if he could open up, at least a little bit, a smidgeon, enough to get to know her better? And, maybe, also to let her presence soothe him?

He knew today of all days, she could use a hand baking or delivering all those new cookies, even if she would have declined his offer of help. Her staff would be gone by now most likely, and she said she had an event-thing to attend later. So this afternoon, for fun, loosely defined, there was one and only one place he knew he had to go.

* * *

While the dough blended to the right consistency, Anna set her rolling pins and guides on the counter, prepped another round of ingredients for multiple kinds and colors of icing. Over the whirring of the mixer, loud banging redirected her attention. *The back door?* It sounded like someone was knocking.

Through the peephole, what she first noticed was a white Santa beard blowing.

Well, not exactly.

What she first noticed was the face that was revealed while the Santa beard caught a gust of wind.

His jawline, the stubble next to the strong cheekbones, the presence in those blue eyes, his masculine lips—goodness, he was more attractive than she remembered.

But who was this strange voice in her head showing so

much interest, she wondered as she unlocked the deadbolt to tell him she was really busy with the baking and didn't have time to chat.

"Anna, I hope this is okay." The blue eyes widened with earnestness and anticipation. "I just finished with the kids and got here as fast as I could. Please, I would really like to help."

She started to say, *I usually prefer to do the baking and decorating on my own so thank you very much, but I don't need a hand.*

Two more hands definitely would make it easier to meet her aggressive schedule, but she didn't think in those terms anymore. Alone was how she had learned to operate since... well, for a long time.

But James' hopeful expression, his handsome face, the sincerity in his eyes, instead she blurted the exact opposite: "Thank you. I could use some backup. It's cramped in here, but make yourself at home."

He stepped inside and she locked the door behind him, careful not to bump his belly. It really was a tiny shop—perfect when she started out but now, especially at this exact moment, she was ready for something larger. Which was why she had submitted her business plan to the Angels all those months ago. And why Siena and Reef worked the front while she baked alone back here. As Blake had told her many times—ironically, after he copped to having an affair—Anna was not the world's most collaborative team player.

Although, the small space wasn't so terrible. It might even have advantages. In a small space one could notice things. Such as people. Male people. Up close. Like their height, say, and the broad set of their shoulders. She had sat next to this particular male person earlier on his throne but had not fully, fully appreciated his build or his scent—a hint of citrus, a note of peppermint—which she might possibly be able to enjoy in such close proximity.

They shimmied around each other as she raised her arms and moved toward the counter, pointing to the wooden coat rack outside her office. "Feel free to hang up your costume and hat and"—she shook her head at the weirdness of this day—"your beard and wig."

When she reached the spot by the counter she was aiming for, she tried to get back to work while she waited for him to change. *What was it again she was doing?*

"How's it going?" He raised his voice so she could hear him over the mixer now that he wasn't standing so close. "I see you already have dough mixing."

"First batch, but there's still a ton to do. I'm trying not to obsess about the time."

"Great!" he said, surprising her with such a positive reaction. "Then it's good I got here when I did."

She made the mistake of looking at him when he spoke and, once she had, she could not turn away. He was unbuckling his wide black Santa belt and taking off the plush red jacket. He hung it up next to his hat while she tried not to fixate on his muscular arms, the swells and curves of the chest muscles, or the way they moved under his T-shirt.

Not fixating.

He unfastened the white strap that encircled his waist, the one attached to his belly padding. "Silicone," he narrated as he undressed. "Jiggles like the real thing." When he nudged it to demonstrate, she couldn't help but laugh.

"Here, let me give you a hand," a familiar woman's voice offered, coming from Anna's vicinity.

She took the few steps toward him and supported the

belly from the bottom with both hands. It was heavy and quite the contraption. It had straps around his waist and mid-back to carry the bulk of the weight, and a halter around his neck to help keep it in place. Together they lifted it off and she held it, the surprising heft forcing her to squat as she set it on the floor, as out of the way as possible behind the coat rack.

In the process, she might have happened to notice that James' real belly did not jiggle.

The soft cotton of his tee was tight around his chest and loose over his stomach. From what she could tell so far, he was... What was the phrase Carli liked to use when talking about gorgeous celebs? That's right: *Cut.*

She needed to get back to work so in order to think about something else, she changed the subject. "How did the rest of the party go? And your visits upstairs?" As soon as she asked that last question, she realized she shouldn't have.

"The rest of the party was a great success, judging from all the laughter and the rousing end of the concert I caught. Oh, and the sleigh—by the time I left it had been totally emptied of gifts. The visits upstairs"—the sadness behind his eyes came forward, and again she regretted having asked —"meeting those kids, going up there, was hard. Can I tell you more about it later instead?"

"Yes, yes, of course. Or not at all if that's better." She reached out and touched the upper part of his arm, the part safely covered by the fabric of his short sleeve. The part that, she happened to notice even with the material between them, was warm and muscular and hard. "I'm sorry I asked—and that it was difficult."

The smile he gave her then, it made her feel woozy. And then it got worse when he put both hands on her shoulders, but close in, more like at the base of her neck. His touch was warm and gentle but firm and, his thumbs, they did this subtle caressing thing. "I appreciate that you asked," he said, leaning his forehead close but still keeping a safe, respectful distance, "and I want to tell you, Anna, I do. But not until after you meet your deadline, when hopefully we'll have more time."

She nodded yes as she caught her breath, and the subtle caressing stopped. Sadly, he took his hands away so he could finish undressing, while she took the dough from the mixer and began to roll it out.

Out of the corner of her eye, she saw him put one hand on the counter to balance as he slipped off his big black shoes and stepped out of the baggy red pants. Underneath, he wore a pair of faded black denim jeans.

Yes, oh my, yes, Santa was definitely cut.

Then he pulled off the beard and the eyebrows, put the gold glasses away in his jacket pocket. Without the glare of the lenses, his eyes, they still held that same glint. And underneath his white wig just as she suspected was a thick tousled mop of salt-and-pepper hair.

Tousled like an invitation to comb your hands through it, not to tame it but to feel the wildness, the disorder.

Tousled like a Sunday morning.

Tousled like a Sunday morning we-can-take-our-time-because-my-kids-are-in-New-York fling.

For example.

She cleared her throat. Maybe that would help wipe the images from her mind. Watching him undress had provided new information to process, given her an expanding idea of him not as Old St. Nick but as a regular... a regular... Her throat seemed to tickle again, so she cleared it one more time. ...not as anything regular but as an incredibly attractive man.

"Shall we?" she asked, pointing to the dough on the counter, although right now with him standing this close, she realized making cookies was the least of what she wanted to do.

Customers!

Okay, focus. He washed his hands, and she gave him a disposable white cap from the box she kept on the shelf. As she handed the cap to him, she pictured how he had so gently lifted her hairnet off earlier at the hospital, how she had closed her eyes to better feel his touch.

Yes, exactly: Focus. Fo-*cus*.

From the edge of the shelf, she unclipped the decoration instructions for the upcoming batches and put them on the counter where he could better see them.

He was experienced, so she didn't have to guide him much; he knew exactly what to do. While she pressed the cookie cutters into the thin sheets of dough, he would grease the next tray and hand it to her as soon as she was ready.

Over the past few years at this time each December, she would catch herself briefly lusting after automated equipment to speed up her production time. But commercial machines were expensive for one thing but also, more importantly, she wanted to make each cookie on her own. That way she could control the exact shape and size to fit her designs and decorations. She was hardly the only cookie baker in the area, and from the start she had the strongest hunch she could distinguish herself from the other shops with two things: her recipes and her custom, personal touch.

Right now, with James working beside her, she was grateful she made the choice to forgo the automation. They worked together easily, a companionable assembly line of two, even better than, dare she say, some mechanical, well-lubricated machine.

Focus.

Finally, the dough was gone, and she slid the last tray into the oven. "There!" she said excitedly at the achievement, as he raised his palm to give her a high-five.

"Well done, Anna."

"Mostly because you helped." She squeezed his hand. "Thank you."

"My pleasure. What's next?"

"While the cookies bake, I need to call one customer again, the only one I couldn't reach. Then I'll start mixing another batch of dough. If you want, you can prepare the rest of the icing."

"Consider it done, milady." He crossed one arm over his abs—*stomach! why was she still thinking about abs?*—and half-bowed as if she were a royal. She shook her head again, amused at his goofy humor, and disconnected her phone from the charging cable.

Guy's voicemail picked up after four rings, and instead of leaving another message she ended the call, tapped out another text, and pressed send.

When she connected the phone again and laid it back on the counter to keep charging, James looked at her over his shoulder. "No luck, I take it?"

"Voicemail. So I texted. Again." The situation was not giving her a great feeling. "He's a good customer. He's also wealthy and influential, and his wife has more social media followers than the entire Orange County population."

The lines across James' forehead dipped in the center as he probably questioned her math. "I'm exaggerating," she said. "But only slightly. I haven't told anyone outside the shop yet—just my employees know—but he is also the managing partner of the O.C. Christmas Angels, which is hosting its Christmas gala tonight. Their private equity fund is a potential investor for a second bakery location. A few months ago, I submitted my business plan and gave a pitch to the group as part of a competition. I was invited to the gala—that's the event I told you about earlier—which means I was selected as a finalist. Tonight, they announce who will get their investment funding."

"Whoa, Anna! That's amazing. I fully expect that tomorrow morning I'll be having coffee with the winner."

"I don't know about that. I haven't won yet, but..." She looked at him and those eyes of his, they gave her the sense she could voice things she would not otherwise say out loud. "I'm hopeful. I don't know the other small businesses that also entered—I'm sure they're all good candidates—but my plan and the financial forecasts are strong, and Guy knows my product; he's been a customer almost since the first day I opened the door."

"I'm hopeful too, and don't worry, my lips are sealed." He made a motion by his mouth like he was turning a key. Her focus shifted from his...mid-section, the stomach area... to his lips.

Dough!

She trusted that he would keep the details confidential, so she told him more about her vision. He listened and nodded while they worked, interested. She poured dry ingredients into the large floor-mixer bowl, and using her best countertop stand mixer, he made the royal icing. When he asked her, "How do you dry it?", her heart must have skipped at least two beats. Never in her wildest dreams would she have imagined a man would ask her this. It was a question that showed a more-than-basic level of knowledge and, more importantly, engagement; it showed that, unlike Blake for example, he actually gave a damn.

She pointed to the fan standing in the corner, covered with a custom canvas tarp to prevent it from gathering dust that would ruin the icing designs. Without her saying anything, he released the brake on the rolling rack she kept nearby and slid it into position. He put it in just the right spot, perfectly aligned. Her mind began to wander but quickly she pulled it back, thinking instead of the cookies that would shortly need to be iced.

While the dough took a few more seconds to combine, she assembled the rest of the icing bags, knives, toothpicks, and brushes, and he laid them out neatly on the counter, organized in the precise order they would need them. Plus tweezers and the vial of gold flakes for the runners and dashboard of a Santa sleigh and the yacht string lights. Then they assembled the boxes and the covers and stacked them on the counter in the corner, ready to receive the contents.

As soon as they unfolded the last box, he leaned back against the counter and eyed her slyly, but she already recognized his playful look and so she guessed he was about to tease her. "So, when I got here, I peeked through the archway and saw your amazing decorations out front—the golden twinkly lights draped across the front window, your cedar boughs along the glass case, and the massive pine cones hanging from the ceiling—they could give Bigfoot a concussion."

She covered her mouth to stop her laugh from coming out too loud. "It looks like an elegant lounge in a posh mountain resort," he continued, "and you obviously went to a lot of trouble to create a cozy, welcoming atmosphere for your customers and staff. So I can't figure it out." He toyed with his chin as if pondering a critical question. "Tell me, Anna, why is it you hate Christmas?"

Chapter 7
in the flesh

There was her name again—not fair—and his question hit her from left field. She looked at him, surprised. "Why do you ask? I don't hate Christmas. Why on earth would you think that?"

"Okay, fair enough. Maybe 'hate' is too strong a word. 'Dislike'? 'Averse to'? You traffic in nuts, so maybe 'allergic to'? I know it's not because you have to make a ton of cookies—watching you, it's clear you love to bake."

She shot him a sidelong smile, but still she was confused. "I do love to bake. Preferably not under pressure like this, but otherwise yes—cookies especially, I do."

That was why she had decided to start her own business, instead of banging her head against a wall trying to find another job teaching art after she and Blake split. Apparently she had been out of the workforce for too many years raising their kids. When it came time to choose a company name, she had asked Ben and Carli for input, and for days they batted around a bunch of silly ideas. Until one of them suggested they play off alphabet letters and their first initials: A, B, C. Anna's Bakery of Cookies was born.

As soon as she turned the mixer off, James lowered his voice. "So you love to bake, but you are...displeased...with Christmas?" His crooked smile and two dimples—one adorably higher than the other—surrounded by the five o'clock shadow that gave his face a rugged look, were more appealing than she could let herself think about. Those dimples were especially heartening after how sad he had looked at the hospital.

"I. Do. Not. Hate. Christmas." But even though she laughed as she said it, her volume had gone up—not to a yell, more like when Reef was vacuuming the front of the shop and Anna would try to talk over the noise to the kids on the phone—and it kind of might sound like maybe she was not so crazy about Christmas. "The thing with Christmas is..."

She hesitated; she wasn't the type of person to insta-share with strangers. But he was not a stranger anymore, was he? The hum in the air between them didn't feel like the energy of a stranger. Besides, he was standing here, in front of her, in the flesh—firm, muscular flesh—helping her fix the mess, and he had asked a reasonable question in an effort to get to know her.

Or more likely, Anna, just to make polite conversation.

Either way, as she spoke, she looked at him, noticed the smudge of icing beside his nose. Without thinking, she stepped close and gently wiped it away. She wanted to lick her finger, taste the sugar from his skin, but they were baking, and that was not exactly in keeping with health department regulations.

His breath caught when she touched him, or maybe it had been hers. Regardless, some invisible barrier crumbled. His gaze remained on her, his eyes ready to listen to what-ever she would say.

"The thing with Christmas," she started again, "is just that, I really miss my kids." It wasn't any deep dark confession, more a simple truth. "They're with their father and his new wife, doing things we used to do as a family. I don't miss him; I don't want to get back together. But being without the kids at the holidays is hard, and when they're not here, it just doesn't feel like Christmas, you know?"

Those eyes of his were empathetic; he hadn't needed to say "I get it" for her to tell he could relate.

"How about you?" she asked. "You obviously don't hate Christmas—I mean anyone who invests in the super-deluxe silicone belly padding can't hate it." She patted her own belly to illustrate as she spoke. "But playing Santa probably isn't part of your chef job description."

Just then, the back door rattled against the metal frame even though it was locked; the wind, she could hear it gusting through the ventilation system; it must have picked up outside again.

He paused before answering, maybe noticing the wind himself, or maybe he didn't want to say. Maybe the answer had something to do with what he said he would tell her later. She began to raise her hand to let him know it was fine not to share, but now he was starting to speak. "I wanted to volunteer as Santa at the hospital for a while, but...I couldn't." She felt her forehead tighten, wondering why not, but again she didn't ask, didn't want to pry.

"My kid got sick a few years ago and the three of us—Noah and my now ex-wife Claire and I—spent a December there. The people were amazing. They made the weeks we had left incredibly meaningful. I wanted to do something in return, and I actually promised one of the staff I would play Santa for the kids one day. It took me a while, until today in fact, to make good on that commitment. I guess I needed more time."

He crossed his arms, then put his hands back where they had been, resting on the counter behind him. "When the chef job in the kitchen opened up this spring, I don't know...it seemed like it could be a safe way to come back. I would be working in a totally different part of the hospital so I figured I wouldn't see any kids, or anyone else I knew from back then. And I was right—I don't. But just being here again and remembering all the kindness, it was enough for me to know this was the year for me to try the Santa thing. At least once."

"I'm so sorry. I can't imagine..." She could barely say the words aloud, "losing a child."

Here she was complaining about missing her kids to someone whose child was not going to bang through the door on New Year's Day after their vacation, blast their music, dump their dirty laundry, roll their teenage eyes. Playing Santa all afternoon, talking and laughing with child after child, it had to have rebroken his heart.

Speaking of rebreaking his heart, she remembered how she snapped at him earlier as they walked to his Santa chair. How when he said it was "just cookies," she asked him, sharp and condescending, if he had kids. And then she remembered how he looked stunned before he answered, so softly she could barely hear him, *no*.

"Oh, James, I owe you a *huge* apology." She took a step forward and turned, so she was standing beside him, her back also to the counter. Then she leaned against his side, wove one arm through his, and softly touched the front of his shoulder by his bicep. "I am very sorry I asked you so harshly if you had kids before, and then I lectured you about what it was like to take care of them. You know more about caring for a child when it most matters than me, and I am just so sorry about how that must have sounded to you, how it must have hurt you."

She wanted to ask him what happened, specifically how he had been able to cope, but she trusted he would tell her more when, or if, he felt safe opening up. She had not exactly given him a reason to trust her with disclosure.

"It's okay," he said, putting his hand on top of hers. Then he pressed it harder. "I have to get used to people asking that question. Since it happened, other than work—actually, including at work—I keep to myself, and that's in large part why. It's basically impossible to answer. Saying yes invites more questions, but saying no, that's almost harder, like it doesn't acknowledge that he was here. To be honest, the way you were speaking to me at the time, no was the easier choice. I didn't want to share difficult personal details with you."

"I'm surprised you're talking to me now at all, much less helping with the cookies. That was so terrible of me. Obviously, I had no idea, but it doesn't matter. I shouldn't have spoken to you like that. I'm so sorry again. I hope you can forgive me."

His hand moved from the top of hers to the side of her face. A gentle caress that told her he did. "It's okay, Anna. You had no way of knowing what happened. And also, you donated so many cookies, I figured you couldn't be that bad a person. Despite evidence to the contrary." There was that uneven-dimpled smile again.

She apologized once more, and he told her to stop saying she was sorry. "By the way, what you said before, that you can't imagine? You're wrong, Anna, you can. You're a parent. It's what you feel right now, the missing. Only it gouges deeper into your soul and, I don't know quite how to describe it, it's heavy, like a boulder you can't heave off your chest, and it never goes away."

The numbers on the oven display indicating temperature and remaining bake time blurred, and she wiped her eyes. She also wiped the tears that had started to fall down her cheek, and as she did, she thought it was good she hadn't maimed him, that he was a kind and sensitive man, resilient and forgiving. Good-looking on top of it all, and...

There was that gusty, metallic rattle once more as the back door clattered against the frame and air whipping through the ductwork howled.

The overhead lights flickered and, to her horror, the ones in the oven did too.

Once.

Twice.

And then all of the lights in her shop—*all* of the lights—they went completely out.

Chapter 8
dark moment

Her eyes popped wide and her whole expression, it fell like a ruined soufflé. In the low light, James could still make out the dawning of recognition on her face. The electric hum of normal, everyday life ceased, and in the noticeable silence he felt her shock in his gut, a left hook to the ribs.

She was still standing beside him, but she unhooked her arm from his and stared at the oven. "Please do not tell me the electricity just went out."

She pushed off the counter and stepped toward the tall, dark appliance. He followed and, standing behind her, placed his hands on her shoulders—crisis or not, he didn't want to let go of her. "It will probably come back on in a second." Although immediately he thought better of making optimistic predictions. "A couple of minutes," he revised. "Stay calm. Just give it a few minutes. I promise, I'll keep track of the time."

He looked at his watch and made a mental note.

"It can't be out," she said. "The cookies..."

"I know." He was nodding behind her, as if willing his

estimation to be true. "Let's give it a couple of minutes. *Ten*. Ten minutes. My guess is by then the problem will resolve itself."

He felt her shoulders drop in resignation and he caught himself starting to massage them but quickly stopped. Instead, he turned her around to face him. "Staring at it won't help. Is there anything else we need to do that doesn't require power?"

"Everything is done except for the baking, the one, you know, kind of critical step." She was shaking her head, as if she still couldn't believe it. She ran to the front door, unlocked it and looked out in both directions, and then she turned back toward him. "The lights down the whole block seem out. The tattoo parlor has a neon sign that's usually on 24/7, and it's not lit now. But maybe the pizza place around the corner..."

When her cell phone rang from its spot on the counter, their heads both whipped around in unison to look. "Power!" she whispered. "Can you check the circuit breakers?" she asked, pointing toward the panel by the back door. "Maybe we only blew a fuse."

Again, he watched her facial expression change as she realized that the phone, unlike the oven or the mixer or the overhead lights, had a battery.

"Right. Not a fuse." She unplugged the phone from the cable and although she said, "Hi, Honey," as upbeat as she could, he could hear the tightness in her voice.

"I'll check anyway," he said softly, gesturing toward the gray fuse panel. Maybe he could fix this somehow; it would be nice to have magical powers. For a lot of reasons but, right now, after seeing the defeat in her eyes when that oven went dark, he wished like crazy for something he could do. He felt oddly protective of her. And it was dawning on him that this odd, protective feeling might not only be because the mess she—they—were in right now was pretty much totally and completely all his fault. Maybe this funny feeling was caused by something else.

She nodded as she spoke to...he glanced at the screen on his way to the fuse box and saw a teenage likeness of Anna, so he figured it must be her daughter.

"Is anything wrong?" Anna asked.

"No, mom, everything is great!" said her excited voice through the speaker.

"Okay, good. I want to hear about it, but I'll have to call you back in a little while—I'm at the bakery and in a bit of a jam right now."

"But mom, it's impooortant," James heard her say—or whine, it sounded more like.

"Then call me back in a couple of minutes and don't use video—my battery hardly has any charge."

Anna ended the call as James came to stand beside her. "Sorry," he pointed toward the fuse box. "It would have been an easy fix, but the power is definitely out."

"I know." She plugged the useless charging cable back into her phone and raised her hands as if she were asking, *why?*

Then she leaned against the counter and brought her hands to cover her eyes. "I really can't believe this. What am I supposed to do?"

"I don't know, I..." he instinctively put his hand on his forehead, as if that would give him the rest of the response.

She nodded toward the oven. "How long do you think it will take for them to bake but not dry out while the temperature falls?" There were hundreds of cookies on the racks inside; that oven was totally full.

"Honestly? No idea."

"My laptop is in my office," she said automatically, "but... Right." They both voiced it at the same time: "No wifi."

"And I don't have a smartphone," he said, suddenly angry at himself for not being able to figure a way out of this predicament and embarrassed he hadn't yet joined the twenty-first century. He hardly communicated with anyone; his circle had shrunk so much. Except for work stuff and Claire's routine couple of annual calls, even his old flip phone, he rarely used it.

"It's okay." But clearly it wasn't. Simultaneously, she clutched her elbows protectively and bit the side of her lip. "I guess I'll call the customers and let them know. I can make the calls from the van."

"Good thinking," he said, but she was already on her way out the door. And then almost as quickly, she marched back in.

He saw it by her hip, even before she raised her hand to show him, a frayed charging cable with wires sprouting through the worn black coating, nearly disconnected from the connector head.

Her eyes grew watery as she looked at him, like she was about to cry. "Just not showing up with customers' orders? Ghosting them on Christmas Eve? It only takes one angry person to share on social media and, that's it for my bakery."

That look on her face, her body language, the tears he could tell she was valiantly holding back, they pained him. Because it was getting easier for him to read the feelings, her feelings: disappointment and its far meaner cousins, defeat, hopelessness, and despair.

"My phone is charged. Partially. You can use that too." The thing was so ancient the battery was draining faster every day, but it would at least help her make a few more of her calls. It was not much, but it was something he could offer.

"Thank you," she said with a smile that flickered as quickly as the lights in the oven a few minutes ago.

Dang, that blasted wind. "Anna. I am so sorry again. You—we—wouldn't be in this situation if I hadn't messed up the cookies in the first place. I feel awful."

"James, I'm saying it again: Stop apologizing. What's done is done. Wrecking the cookies was an accident." She actually laughed then. A resigned and dark laugh but even so it reached her eyes and relaxed her face and he knew it would ever so slightly improve how she was feeling.

"Come here," he said, surprising himself by reaching out to her. She immediately moved closer, and he put his hands on her shoulders again, where they met the delicate skin of her neck.

It seemed different this time, like in the course of only a few short hours, the two of them had...connected. And when she looked up at him with those crestfallen brown eyes, it felt like something in his chest was softening—cold, frozen brick into butter thawing on a sunny counter.

"Hey. Let's try something. Breathe with me. Take a deep breath in," he said, doing the same thing himself. Dr. Washingtonn had suggested this to him and also to Claire one of the few times she joined him for a session. Claire had thought it was dumb, but he did it once in a while, if only to distract himself from...everything...for a few minutes or, make that a few seconds.

As Anna inhaled, she closed her eyes, a simple trusting act that made him imagine caressing the smooth, thin skin of her eyelids with the pads of his thumbs. But he didn't because he was trying to calm her down, and stroking her lovely eyelids might interrupt that. He suspected she wouldn't be upset or offended but still, right now they were simply, platonically, breathing.

Together.

Platonically.

"And breathe out." He let out his own long exhale, enjoying the effect of the loosening. He hadn't felt this sense of...ease? in a long time. Since, well, since Before.

"Again," he whispered near her ear. "Inhale." Her shoulders rose slowly underneath his hands. "And exhale."

He watched her for a second, glimpsing the slightest curve of her lips. "It's not helping so much, is it?" he asked.

"Not so much. A little? Honestly, no. But thanks for trying." As she spoke, he felt his own grin.

"Maybe it's my technique," he said. "I don't really meditate."

"Me either. But I should." Now her shoulders wobbled as she laughed and, for as long as he lived, he would not forget the feeling—an actual good, warm feeling—course through his body as she leaned against him so he could wrap his arms around her and pull her close.

* * *

He rested the side of his head on hers. He smelled so good, not like cologne, but fresh, like citrusy laundry soap with a drop of mint, and maybe also almond, extract. Unlike Blake, who slathered himself in aftershave, James didn't strike her as a fake-smell kind of man. And James' body, with his sculpted chest and strong arms around her, arms deliberately, generously offering support, he made her feel safe. His scent was her aromatherapy; his body, her temporary harbor in this blustery wind shit-storm.

She placed her hand on his chest, felt the curve of his

pecs and, although she hadn't intended to touch him there, noticed his nipple harden beneath the fabric. He moved his hand from around her back to the side of her face and his palm, it sweetly cupped her chin.

His touch was gentle as well as provocative and stirring; it was as if the sensation lifted her face. He must have felt it too because at the same time he lowered his.

Their lips met softly, slowly, and it was a mind-bendingly, perfect, tender, arousing—yes, definitely arousing—kiss.

"Anna," he breathed out in a deep sigh. "Lovely Anna."

The air tickled her top lip and she brought her hand to his warm cheek. His stubble prickled her palm, and she dragged her thumb back and forth along his jaw to feel the sensation again. "This could be a good way to pass the time while we wait those few minutes for the power to come back." His whisper by her mouth made her skin tingle, not just the skin on her face, but her skin pretty much everywhere.

Her mobile rang again just then. "I should get it. It's probably Carli. But this was..." she hated to break away from their embrace, but the call threw her back to reality. "... nice."

Nice did not do it justice—neither how he held her nor that unbelievably gentle, sexy kiss—but her few seconds of bliss were now over, and that was that.

She went to the counter and glanced at the phone screen before hitting the speaker button. "Hey, Car. Tell me, what's going on?"

"Mom! Dad got himself and Ben sold-out box seats for the Christmas Eve Big Apple Buckets game tonight, and Madison's taking me to the Tiegan E. concert! Front row! And a backstage pass for after!"

Anna had looked into taking Carli to see Tiegan E. when he was going to play the Hollywood Bowl, but the cost of the tickets...just the basic seats and not front row... were through the roof. On the website, she had also seen the premium seats and backstage pass pricing. At the time she wondered, *Who actually buys those?*

Even though she should have been able to guess.

"That's amazing, Honey!" She forced her cheeks into a smile although they weren't in video mode. For Carli's sake, she wanted to sound enthusiastic. "You love him. Send me a photo, and tell Ben too, and have a fantastic time! I hate to rush off but the power went out at the..."

Carli sighed, and Anna pictured the eye roll at the same time she braced herself for the instantaneous mood flip. "I know, mom. You're at the bakery. The bakery. The bakery. You're just jealous that we can do fun things with Dad and even on Christmas Eve—every year—you're stuck at the stupid bakery."

Where, exactly, did that come from? Surprise turned into anger and a renewed flash of panic about the power as Anna thought about all the ways her *stupid* bakery helped Carli and Ben have a secure, stable upbringing. That didn't depend on the whims of someone else, like for instance, Blake.

"Careful, Carli. I am truly happy you're going to the concert, but I have an emerg..." And then, because of course, the battery died.

She shook her head, slid the phone onto the counter, looked at James and felt again like she would cry from sheer frustration.

And he was right there, putting those arms around her once more. This time he kissed the top of her head.

"She can be such a brat sometimes," Anna started to tell him, "but it feels awful to hang up mad."

"I know," he said, rubbing her back. "You're welcome to use my phone to call her back."

"I should save the battery to call the clients, but it's my kid."

"Kids, even temporarily bratty ones, overrule clients. But maybe there's enough juice so it won't be an either-or decision."

He handed her the phone, and she flipped it open, noticing he had two missed calls as she pressed the keys for Carli's number. When she picked up, her voice sounded unsure, and Anna recalled the pre-smart-phone-era and that sense of curiosity at answering to hear an unknown caller.

"Have a great time tonight, and we'll talk about this more when you get home," Anna said immediately. "I love you, kiddo."

"Love you too, mom. And sorry. I shouldn't have said that about the bakery. Good luck tonight—you have your competition-gala thing. I know you're going to win."

Anna's chest swelled with love and maternal pride, not at the vote of confidence but the apology and the fact that Carli actually remembered the event. This is why Anna had opened the bakery—to support them and their future—and why she could not fail now. Blake's generosity was over the top, inappropriate in Anna's eyes, and it was also inconsistent, which only confused the kids.

"Hold on," Carli was saying, "Dad wants to talk to you."

Before she could respond, Blake was speaking. "Anna, Madison said I should ask you. I'm getting Carli that smart watch she wants."

Anna glanced at James, whose otherwise handsome face was wrinkling in disbelief.

"That sounds like telling, not asking. And is this before or after the insanely-priced concert tickets?"

"What's the problem, Anna?"

"Could you choose one gift, or at least space them out, wait on the other until her birthday or something? She's gotten..." Anna paused. She hated using labels and especially with her kids and especially negative ones. But the truth was the truth. "...spoiled."

"You're accusing *me* of spoiling her? Last time I checked, she had two parents."

"No Blake, I'm not *accusing* you. I'm just saying she doesn't need an over-the-top concert *and* an over-the-top watch on the same day. She has a phone, a tablet, a laptop, a large-screen TV in her room. She takes a lot for granted, and she's not so appreciative sometimes. If you spent time with her every day, waking her up in the morning, cleaning up after meals, walking away from the outbursts—you know, all the not-fun parts of living together as a family—you might notice. It's easy to play super-dad when it's for a couple of weeks a year on vacation. And when you have the money to buy everything she wants."

Such a hero.

He was quiet for a second, and his pause gave Anna the craziest thought. Maybe for once something she said got through his thick head and he might—*might*—even see her point.

The gusts outside rattled the bakery door again, reminding her she could wish: Maybe winds of change were also blowing in New York.

"Anna," he said more softly now, "I don't want to argue."

Miracles were possible. "Me either. I..."

"We're standing outside and it's cold, so I'm hanging

up," he bulldozed right over her. "We're at the Spiralo store, and it closes in five minutes."

* * *

"He is *quite* the charmer," James said, more sarcastically than he meant to while she flipped his crappy old phone closed and handed it back to him.

"Oh, he certainly is. By the way, you have a couple of missed calls."

James felt his gaze fall and hoped she would let him ignore that news. He put the phone down and with his other hand, took her wrist and gently pulled her in. "After that conversation, Santa thinks you could use a hug."

That got her to smile, at least partially, and when she put her arms around him, he felt her grab hold of her other wrist behind his lower back, like she was getting comfortable. "Are the calls always like that?" he asked.

"More or less, unfortunately. They seem to bring out the best in each other. He's an adult, technically speaking, but Carli, I just hope one day the values and the skills I try to teach her will get through."

"I don't have experience with teenagers—Noah was only four"—Anna let go of her wrist and raised her arms to soothingly rub his back. It was the second time today he had said Noah's name out loud. Anna, something about Anna, it made him want to share it. "But I believe you just have to keep trying, especially when you see a good opportunity, and beyond that, I guess all you can do as a parent is hope."

"You're right, and I plan to bring this up with her at a better time. I always do. If I catch her at the right moment, I can see the wheels turning, like what I'm saying is getting through"—Anna pointed to her head, and he immediately missed the pressure of her palm on his back. "Most of the time, she's a good kid, so I know she does pay attention."

Anna was quiet for a second, and then she spoke again. "I really..." She shook her head, like she wasn't sure how to finish the thought, but he stayed quiet, watching her think, smelling the floral scent of her hair, wanting to hear what she would say next. Not just what she would say about her jerk of an ex or raising a kid but about anything. He could listen to her, and watch her pretty face—preferably from up close, like while he was holding her—for any amount of time.

"...about my ex, you must wonder, how stupid could I have been?" While she spoke, she stared at the dark oven. "He wasn't like this when we got together and early on in our marriage. Or maybe I just didn't see it, but..."

"It's kind of hard to miss," they both said, again finishing the other's sentence at the same time. He liked how they did that, how they knew without thinking what the other was about to say and also, that there was no lingering resentment between them, be it over mundane things or larger but unmet expectations.

"What happened?" he asked.

"Good question. It's hard to say exactly how relationships devolve—so many unintended slights over time and less talking, and I think people also change," she was saying. "You hope you're with someone who's committed to making it work but for Blake, obviously that wasn't the case."

James shook his head because he could appreciate what she was saying, although the devolution was different for him and Claire.

"What I struggle with still," she went on, "is how suddenly and independently he decided to give up. We weren't perfect together—what couple is?—but his affair was a shock; I had not suspected a thing. Now, the whole idea of partnership? It feels like a bad idea."

"Hear, hear," James said heartily agreeing, but a tinge of doubt and also disappointment flicked at him once the words were out. Was that really true, that all relationships were destined to fail?

He could tell from the slightest drop of her eyes that she noticed his internal dissonance. And then she quickly diverted the discussion. "Speaking of disasters, how long has it been now?"

He looked at his watch although he already knew. "Barely five minutes."

She started to pull away, but he caught her forearms, looked down at her tense but still beautiful face. "We said we'd give it ten, remember?"

She leaned against him again in an instant, and her chest pattered against his torso. Feeling her laugh made him smile. The connection between them was something he could feel in the air, and—strangely, because it was new—with all of his senses. They were heightened, more attuned, as much as that made no rational sense. He had known Anna only a handful of hours, so how was it possible? He hadn't noticed it with any woman before, not even his former wife.

He understood now why people described it as electric. Although that seemed like a cruel analogy at this particular moment.

Now Anna was shaking her head against his chest. "I really can't believe this," she said. "The Christmas Angels' contest was super-competitive to begin with, and if I can't deliver to the managing partner, I can kiss goodbye any chance of winning."

James leaned back, took her face in his hands. "Don't go

there yet. It's only been five minutes, and twenty-two seconds."

"You're right, I know, I need to stay in the present. It's just that—damn it!" This time as she pulled away, he didn't draw her back. "I started over after Blake announced he was leaving. Started over from the ground up—emotionally and financially, while taking care of the kids and starting the business. I made a promise to myself and, without their knowing it, to the kids: that I would never let us be that exposed, vulnerable, or at someone else's mercy again. So I cannot fail at this, James. I can't."

He shrugged.

It was involuntary, and the absolutely worst possible reaction to the belief she just shared. Flames practically combusted in her eyes.

"Anna, don't be angry—please, trust me, I'm not minimizing what's going on."

He got it about feeling abandoned and discarded, about heartbreak and failure and disappointment, about the plans you imagined—that you dreamt of—not working out.

"But life comes with no guarantees. You might fail—not you yourself but the business, although I don't think that's going to happen. But for argument's sake, let's say it does."

She crossed her arms in front of her, protective, and he didn't reach out to stop her as he kept on talking. "And failing will have to be okay, because here's the thing: We only have the present. And right now, we have no cookies to deliver, and currently there is no power. Short of building a fire in your oven, which is not a great idea for many reasons, there is not so much we can do."

He felt her body relax against him just a hair. He wondered if it was because, he realized, he had said *we*, not *you*.

"Everything you're saying is very wise, but I can't put myself or the kids in that position again."

"Anna, believe me, there is only so much you can influence. Besides, your kids are incredibly lucky. You'll always be a great mom who puts them first. With that fierce love and protectiveness, even if the bakery were to close tomorrow and you had to restart again, you'd do it; you'd find another solution. And in the process, you would teach them by example some valuable life lessons."

He tightened his arm around her, wanting to make her feel safe—one arm around her back, his hand resting on her shoulder, the other arm around her waist. And then he rocked her, gently side to side, rested his chin on the top of her head. The hair net tickled his skin while he inhaled the scent of her contained but noticeably still-soft hair.

He wanted to take the net off again like he had at the hospital, see her wavy locks fall around her shoulders, run his fingers through it, really mess it up. "Everything will be okay," he whispered. "It will." He almost added *I promise,* but he had said that to Claire once, trying to reassure them both, and he had unfortunately been very wrong.

Her lips parted and she took a breath as if about to speak.

"Only ten seconds have passed since the last time you checked. Do I need to distract you again?"

Her smile was like a heater in a blizzard, and it sent more of his blood pulsing southward. That he was wearing jeans, rather than the baggy Santa pants, helped contain his enthusiasm; it kept a certain awkwardness from arising between them.

But then she placed her palms on his sides just above his waist and then ducked them under his shirt. Her touch was enlivening, and he read it as her agreement for distraction. With a slight lift of his index finger he tipped her chin, bent his head to meet her lips.

As their mouths came together, as he took her full, soft lower lip between his, she made the quietest, sexiest sound, a pleasurable little gasp. That noise inspired him, and the kissing intensified. He tried not to overthink or take his attention away from this moment, but it was hard to deny that she was awakening a long-dormant part of his heart.

While they explored, he couldn't help it, he touched her face, his thumbs skimming her cheekbones, where he could feel her faintly smile. "What's wrong?" he asked, suddenly worried he might be out of practice, or that his technique was out of date. "Is something funny?"

"Nothing's wrong," she sighed. "These kisses, they're nearly perfect. But I thought of a dumb joke. Because I think I'm a little nervous."

"Don't be nervous," he said on a whisper, as he languidly moved from her lips to peck the tip of her nose. "What's the silly joke?"

She initiated the next kiss, almost like she wanted to avert her gaze, and at the same time slowly drew her hands down his sides and inward toward his navel. His body did not find humor in the sensuousness or the direction of her movement. "Is that a rolling pin in your pocket," she murmured against his lips, "or are you just glad to see me?"

"Oh, Anna," he chuckled, less embarrassed than he expected. "If I may humbly insert myself into your temporary crisis, besides being a kick-ass mom and a smart businessperson, you're also an incredible, like, super-incredible kisser. So no, that's not a baking implement in my pocket, it's what you do to me."

"Mmm," she uttered, smiling with closed eyes. "I know

the feeling—I haven't kissed like that in...years. Or, actually, maybe ever."

She began to drag her fingertips further down his happy trail, and he imagined her dipping them lower, to feel his contours through the denim. But she stopped herself, brought her arm to her side while curling her shoulders forward and flashing him a sheepish grin. "Sorry," she said, "I can't lose focus. Now how long has it been?"

Chapter 9
half-baked

James turned his wrist to see the watch face, and as much as he wanted to be optimistic and stay calm for her, he had to admit the situation was starting to look dire.

"Seven minutes."

"Seven minutes," she repeated. "Shoot. I can't wait any longer. We need to get those trays out."

"If you insist. Because me, I'm still hopeful. And otherwise we could kiss for two minutes and fifty-eight seconds."

"We can't. Time's up. We need to move to plan b."

"Okay, boss," he sighed, putting on a pair of heat-resistant mitts. "Hold on, Anna. What about the hospital kitchen?"

For a second, she seemed to consider it. "It's a good idea but impractical to transport the trays that far, and it would probably also break some institutional rule—I wouldn't want you to get in trouble. Thanks for the offer, but I'll drive around the neighborhood, quick. There's the pizza place and a vegan café around the corner. Maybe one of them is open, and their oven's working."

"I'll take care of the trays," he told her, waving a silicone glove. "Go. Get out of here."

Carefully he removed the baking sheets from the oven one at a time and set them in neat rows on the counter. The cookies had just started to glisten from the melting butter in the dough; they were not even half-baked.

As he took off the mitts, he noticed her printout with the orders sitting nearby, so he double-checked that the two of them had unfolded and stacked enough boxes and lids, which they had. And then he confirmed it twice more again.

He absolutely hated this helpless feeling; he wished for something he could do to change it. But if Noah's illness had taught him any sort of lesson, it was that in the grand scheme of things, we possess precious little control. Planning and preparation are important, but they have their limits. Beyond them, he had yet to figure out what else to do besides let go.

And right now he couldn't think of what else to do until Anna returned with, he hoped, good news.

He didn't intend to snoop, but that kiss had aroused, among other things, his curiosity. In chronological order starting with their crash, he catalogued his knowledge: He knew she was beautiful. He knew she was generous, otherwise she would not donate cookies, so many cookies, to the hospital. He knew she didn't want her ex-husband back but, especially at Christmastime, she missed her kids. He knew she was determined, while also sweet and down to earth. That her lips were as warm and comforting as hot cocoa. That how she looked at him and touched him with her delicate hands, really, like really, turned him on.

He peeked around the wall to her office. A bulletin board hung on the short wall, pinned with a five-dollar bill and some newspaper and magazine articles with baking puns for titles: *Smart Cookie, Knead Cookies?, Sweet Second Career.*

He moved closer to see the others. There was a glossy magazine piece about opening day and a business newspaper article with a picture taken under the green and white awning of Anna and, based on the caption, her employees Siena and Reef. Next to that was pinned a thank-you note and autograph on a photo of a celebrity whose face James recognized but whose name escaped him.

Her desk was small to fit the tiny space, the surface as neat as he would have expected. A laptop, a small printer, pens standing in a pink mug with a crooked handle. It must have been handmade by one of her kids, Carli he guessed by the color. To its left sat a trophy of a figure kicking a soccer ball on a square of marble, the base engraved with Ben's name. A jade plant grew in a tiny white pot, and to the right was a plate stand propping up a flat, round Christmas ornament.

Holy crap, James heard himself whisper as his eyes bugged out.

The red ribbon tied through the top hole, the unevenly raised edge, the depressions from a child's finger pad pressed around the lip. And the smooth, brown melted chocolate-chip spots with the blurred edges, they appeared in the exact same places as the ones he remembered on the small Santa Christmas cookie plate in Dr. Washingtonn's office.

He should know because as he sat on her couch five years ago trying to make sense of what was happening, he had stared at it no end, a beacon in the gray of a standard-issue metal desk. It had given him a place to rest his swollen eyes, because sometimes making visual contact with another person was too much. One time when she noticed him looking at it, she told him her granddaughter had made it for her, that every Christmas she, her daughter, and her granddaughter baked cookies for Santa together.

From what he knew of Anna's life so far, she and Dr. Washingtonn—Lucy, she had said to call her—had two things in common: baking cookies at Christmas and the hospital. He tried to picture Dr. Washingtonn's face. All day looking at Anna, he hadn't thought she looked familiar, but reconsidering now, maybe, yes, he could see a faint resemblance.

He would ask Anna about this as soon as she got back, as soon as their baking crisis was over. He went to the counter, checked to make sure nothing terrible had happened to the cookies resting on the trays. What that catastrophe might be at this very second when everything was quiet, he didn't know, but he could not bear another accident on his watch.

She wasn't back when he finished checking and so he resumed his perusal of the space. Baking and cookie cookbooks ran half the length of the shelf above the counter. Recipes, written by hand and laminated, hung from the edge, while framed photos ran the rest of the way to the wall: Anna and two kids in front of the bakery about to cut a big mint-green ribbon; the three of them by the ginormous Christmas tree in...it looked like Rockefeller Center; a little boy sitting on a plush sofa next to Anna, a beautifully decorated tree in the background. A strand of gold tinsel had fallen in her hair. Her gaze was loving, focused on the infant in her arms, probably Carli. In Anna's face, he could see exhaustion, like any parent would recognize. But also, he saw her sense of wonder and sheer unguarded, unafraid delight.

Unafraid.

If a camera lens were turned on the spaces James inhabited, what would they reveal? Mentally, he scanned his desk at work, bare except for strictly job-related items, his furniture-less apartment, the living and bedroom walls with nothing hung on them, the boxes of clothes and books he never bothered to unpack, the dearth of keepsakes.

He pared down every time he moved, which was often given his short-term gigs and restless, nomadic existence. But it was one thing to consciously pursue a life unencumbered by clutter and material possessions; it was another to shun anything that would evoke a memory because in order to protect your decimated heart, you needed to stay disconnected.

The more he learned about Anna, though, the more he admired her. Okay, it was a lot more than admiration; he was in serious like with the picture of the woman who was emerging. Everything she displayed here was meaningful and ultimately centered on her family. Her kids, it was obvious to him they were her raison d'etre. The anger that had scared and repelled him this morning, that led him to run away rather than stay to help her, it looked different to him after spending time with her today.

Now, he understood better; that hostility came from a fierce desire for security for herself and her kids, and given what she had told him about her marriage and what he heard of Blake on speakerphone, it also came from an understandable need for self-preservation.

James got that. He knew the defensive instinct all too well, which was why their spontaneous kiss had come as such a shock. If he had given it any thought, he never would have done it. He had no business extending himself like that or asking it of Anna. But she also must have felt it—the strong pull, the overwhelming sense of familiarity, the crackling attraction, the...hard banging on the door. He ran to the front and saw through the glass a middle-aged man in business attire with a worried, impatient expression.

James unlocked the two deadbolts and stepped back to let him in. "Who are you?" the guy asked but then waved his hand like he didn't have time to wait for an answer. "I need to speak to Anna. My wife just called and said there's been no delivery yet. I was on my way home and thought I better stop by to check. The lights in the shop windows up and down the block are all off. What the heck is going on?"

* * *

As Anna unlocked the van door to get in, she briefly wondered if it would start. Because, why would it? This day was not going at all as she planned when she woke up this morning. Maybe the hard fall she took in that racy dream was a harbinger of trouble or some kind of sign. The only redeeming elements of the past twelve hours had been at the hospital, in the smiles on the kids' faces when they saw her cookies and, although she wasn't going to spend another second thinking about this, making out with James.

She could not indulge the fresh memory, no matter how exhilarating it was, or how sincere, helpful, and under-standing he was turning out to be. A distraction, that's all it was. It might have brought a newfound sense of aliveness to certain parts of her body but still it was a distraction, as simple as that.

Because kissing James ran exactly one-hundred-and-eighty-degrees counter to everything she had told him, to everything she believed. She could not let herself even have a fling because, what she said about not wanting to start over, not wanting to bear all that risk, not wanting her and the kids' stable world upended again? All of that, it applied equally to her personal life as well as to her business.

The neighborhood streets were quiet when she drove around, the shop windows eerily dark. The café was uninhabited, although outside the dry cleaner, she waved to the owner, who stood by the door with his hands on his hips while his polo shirt billowed in the wind. So desperate at this point, she crazily wondered if there might be a way to somehow use residual heat from his clothing steamer to finish baking the cookies.

At the next corner, she slowed to wait in case other cars were also approaching the intersection. The traffic light housing was actively blowing around, but the signal lights themselves were completely out. No one was coming, so she pressed the accelerator. Between the holiday and the power outage, the streets were deserted, and one thing was depressingly clear: No place nearby would have a working oven.

Looping back toward the alley, she parked again by the bakery's back door, and quickly went inside.

Although, duh, Anna. What was she hurrying for?

As soon as she shut the door behind her, she heard it, an agitated male voice that she recognized as Guy's. Its sound starkly contrasted with James', whose warm baritone had been so comforting to hear all day.

"The lights in the shop windows up and down the block are all off. What the heck is going on?"

"The electricity went..." James started to reply just as Anna got to the front of the shop.

Guy looked at her, the skin of his forehead scrunched in confusion. "Anna." The wrinkles relaxed some but not entirely. "You never miss a delivery time; if anything you're always early. When Evelyn called, I grew concerned. I was on my way home and thought I should check to make sure everything is okay. While I'm here, I'll save you the trip—I'll pick up my order and also the orders for the Chakrabartis and the Bensons.

Right. About that.

"Thanks for checking on me. I tried to reach you a few times today—I hope you heard my voicemails and saw the texts."

Earth to Anna: If he had, he wouldn't be standing here, offering to take his neighbors' cookies home.

"I've been tied up all day meeting with the partners and getting ready for the gala." He held up his phone as if to prove his point. "I haven't looked at this thing for hours. Luckily, Evelyn happened to catch me while I was in the car."

Luckily.

"I'm afraid the news I have now is even worse than earlier when I left those messages." She looked at Guy squarely as the three of them stood near the empty glass cookie case. "I'm not going to sugarcoat it. There was an accident this morning and your order was damaged. And then while I was replacing it, the electricity... As you can see, it's out." She tried to stand tall as she spoke, but her posture slumped at the shock on his face.

"Anna. Wow. So you're telling me my cookie order isn't ready?"

"That's right; unfortunately, none of them are."

"How did this happen?" He didn't pause for a response. "What kind of accident ruined so many cookies?"

James took a step forward to take the blame, but she raised her eyebrows at him, urging him to stay quiet.

"I was in a hurry loading my van with the orders, and because I was carrying too many boxes, I stumbled and dropped them." There was no need to implicate James. If she had followed her own rules, stuck to her safety practices, she might have bumped into him still but the damage, at least it would have been more limited.

"Maybe I'm confusing you with another competitor, but when the committee reviewed the business plans and operations manuals, if I remember correctly, you had policies and procedures in place to address disruption, to avoid *precisely* this kind of thing."

"You're right—those were my materials, and I did have those procedures. I *do*," she corrected. "But I was in a hurry to get to the hospital to drop off the cookies I donate to their party—I was running behind after a phone call from my daughter, who's out of town with her father—and I made an exception so I wouldn't be late. But hindsight being what it is, that decision turned out to be a terrible mistake."

Out of the corner of her vision, she noticed James shrink back at that last part.

Guy looked pensive as he probably tried to picture the disaster as she described it unfolding. "This is extremely disappointing."

"I know." She shook her head and couldn't help but cast her gaze down. She wished he was furious, screaming, frothing at the mouth. "Trust me, I know."

His phone rang, or not rang exactly, more like it sounded with Evelyn's voice. "Sweetie, it's me; hurry, pick up. Sweetie, it's me..." Anna wanted to say it was a cute ringtone, but she kept it to herself.

"What do you mean, the bounce house backed out?" Guy said with surprise. "What the...? I know it's really windy, but aren't those things weighed down? There's bad news here too, unfortunately. Anna tells me we have..." he raised his eyes toward her as he spoke into the phone. "That we have no cookies."

Anna heard Evelyn's voice but couldn't make out what she was saying, which was probably good for Anna's sake.

"I know it's a ton of kids and the whole thing is falling apart at the last minute. We'll have to come up with something else to entertain them," Guy said. "Hold on, give me a second to think. I'm on my way to the car. I'll call you right back, but just, let's keep an open mind because, Darling, it looks like we might have to cancel."

He ended the call and glanced at James and then his disappointed gaze rested for a moment longer on Anna. If she might have been about to win the competition tonight, her chances were now less than a snowball's odds of survival in Hades.

"I have to go figure this out," he said. "You already know that attendance at the gala is mandatory for all finalists, so I trust we will still see you later."

Still. She was right—she was not going to win.

He turned and was out the door in a flash. The usually-soothing sound of the tinkling bells that hung from the mechanism mocked this ridiculous situation. As she turned around, James touched the back of her shoulder in silent support and commiseration.

He followed her into the back room and they both looked at the empty oven. For no good reason, she put her hand on its side; now it was hardly even warm to the touch. As she looked at him and let out a sigh, her attention landed on his Santa suit hanging on the coat rack by the door. His gaze followed hers to it, and then they looked at each other right at the same moment.

It was obvious he knew what she was thinking because he nodded—*go for it*—and puffed out his sexy chest. Her unease faded, and she smiled as she sprinted to the front of the shop, unlocked the door, and raced outside.

Exhaust fumes taunted her nostrils as Guy drove away.

"Wait!" she cried, but it was futile.

Until another gust of wind howled and blew down a long, thick piece of evergreen garland from between two nearby lampposts. Studded with heavy aqua and gold ornaments and strings of holiday lights, it landed with a heavy thunk right in front of Guy's screeching tires.

He stopped short and jumped out, while Anna seized the moment.

"Guy!" she screamed, taking off toward him.

The ornaments scraped the street as he began to drag the garland to the curb, and she ran harder to catch up to him before he got back into his car.

At the sound of her voice, his head turned sharply in her direction.

"Don't cancel your party," she huffed as she reached him. "What if you have a Santa on hand to entertain the kids?"

"I didn't rent a Santa, Anna. I rented a bounce house and ordered your cookies."

"Yes, yes I understand. But I know a Santa who's free right now and maybe he can save your party." She pointed toward the shop. "My friend, James... It's a long story. But he's a great Santa—he's got this fabulous costume with"— she stretched her hands out in front of her stomach, a lot like she used to hold her belly when she was pregnant with the kids—"a very jiggly belly, and he is funny and adaptable and excellent with children."

Guy finished dragging the bough to the edge of the street and came back to where she was standing. "Seriously?"

"Seriously." She held up her hand, *scout's honor.*

"What about you? You said he was helping you out. When the power is restored—which, let's hope is soon— won't you need him if you're going to finish in time for the gala? That rule about attendance, you agreed to it when you applied, and we do not make exceptions, even for those who don't win.

She pictured the evening gown hanging in her office, thought of how many times she had replayed the looping fantasy of hearing her name announced, of the pride and excitement she would feel about planning her second loca- tion, of giving her thank-you speech to the selection committee.

The fantasy lurched to a halt. A sick feeling washed over her, dousing her in letdown and inadequacy. After this fiasco, she could dump that daydream straight in the trash along with her bakery full of half-baked dough.

"I remember the rules, and I'll do my very best. But it's possible I might be late or not make it at all. I understand this would mean I void my application, and I hate the thought of that. It in no way reflects my level of commit- ment or how much I appreciate the incredible opportunity for the Angels' consideration, but to be honest, it will all depend on the power."

The sound of a car turning onto the block prompted them both to look. "Hold on," Guy said. "Let me pull over." He hopped in and parked his electric sedan by the curb, then got out again and met her on the side of the street.

"If by some Christmas miracle the power comes back," Anna resumed, "I have to finish baking and decorating orders and make those deliveries. My customers, like you, they've been expecting their cookies."

She briefly thought about asking if she could use his

kitchen rather than wait for electricity here, but his order wasn't the only one, and moving everything would be a logistical nightmare. Nor was it likely to save any time, and the quality would surely suffer.

"They're celebrating Christmas Eve with family and friends," she went on, "and they've been loyal clients since I opened. Baking for them is so much more than a business transaction; it's become a holiday tradition. I *so* want to be at the gala to support the competition and the lucky winner, but finishing those cookies and getting them where they need to be tonight must be my first priority."

Chapter 10
bright spot

The way Anna was gesturing, James knew exactly what she was talking about. The sound of his own laugher surprised him as he stood by the bakery's front window watching her through the glass.

How she was rounding her hand in front of her belly, he could tell she was explaining his Santa padding. Guy's expression changed at that, from skepticism and disappointment—and maybe a touch of anger—to hopefulness and even amusement. *There*, James thought, suddenly feeling... pride. Because today, hanging out with Anna, unlike so many other days, he had identified many emotions.

This might be automatic for some people, and it had been for James in the past as well—being able to, more or less, grok how others feel, including oneself—but since Noah, and according to Claire, he had lost that capability.

And just like his emotional IQ apparently had jumped a notch or two today, the little golden Christmas lights that Anna had hanging festively across the bakery window blinked a couple of times like they were waking up from a nap, and...

He held his breath a few seconds.

They stayed on!

The noise behind him further buoyed his glee—*glee*, there was another, and very unfamiliar, feeling—as the ventilation system whirred back on and at the same time, so did the fan for the oven.

He didn't want to waste a second, so he ran to the back and plugged in their phones to charge. It felt weird in a good way, sort of intimate, to take care of Anna's mobile in addition to his own.

Quickly but carefully he slid the cookie sheets back into the oven, checked the temperature, set the timer for six minutes. This was his best calculation based on their appearance of how much baking time remained before the starches would crystallize and dry them out.

Then he lifted the plastic wrap off the icing bowls and confirmed the supplies were still in the right position. When that was done, he tore to the front, opened the door, and ran outside waving and yelling, "Anna! Anna! The power came back on!"

He reached her and Guy and let her know the cookies were baking again. To Guy she said, "I'll bring James straight over as soon as I finish the orders and start making the deliveries. You'll be stop number one. When the kids get there, you can ask them to be patient, tell them Santa is on his way."

Guy got into his car with a grin on his face, and James saw him press a button on the display, most likely calling his wife.

As soon as James and Anna entered the shop and locked the door, he took hold of her by her shoulders and turned her around. "Come here for just a second," he said. "See? It's all going to work out." He hugged her then, felt her arms tighten around his back. He started to bend his head to kiss her, but when she didn't look up at him, he pecked the top of her forehead instead. Now she did look, and her eyes held less excitement than he expected.

"We shouldn't, James. First of all, the time. And also, we both agree, relationships are a recipe for disaster. I have a teenager full of angst, a business that takes the rest of my time and attention, and I never seem to stop arguing with my ex. In other words, I come with a lot of baggage. So as nice as those kisses were, I think we both have to ask, really, what's the point?"

Her words socked him in the belly, almost made him double over with that familiar sinking feeling. Because, although he wanted to say she was wrong, definitely she was right.

"Okay, no more kissing. Let's table that discussion for another time. But just in case you haven't read the memo, I'm not exactly a paragon of no-baggage virtue. Meeting you today, after being shut down for so long, it's been like—no, *you've* been like—a breath of fresh air, a wake-up call." He put his chin on her head again and exhaled a long, deep breath, as if he had been holding it for years. Which, pretty much, he had. "You, lovely Anna," he whispered.

Her wide eyes, the slight tilt of her head, they conveyed both surprise and...longing? Actually stunned like a deer in headlights might have better described her reaction. He didn't want her to feel uncomfortable and, also, rejection sucked. Isn't that what happened when you got close to someone? Eventually, they left.

So he let her go, took a step back, and said, "Come on, let's not waste another minute. We need to finish baking."

* * *

Her thoughts felt like they had tumbled round and round in the mixer's bowl. The truth was, she wanted to kiss him again, especially in that moment of immense relief that the electricity was back. But just like the nice distraction earlier, that's all it was—one moment's excitement, a brief shared experience, nothing that changed the truth.

Then, what he said, about tabling the kissing discussion, like he saw some sort of future that required more talking? Her mind had started down that path as well until she smartly yanked it back. She could not think about that right now, or even later. A relationship? *Pfff.* Definite non-starter.

When the oven timer went off, he helped her take the baking sheets out and slide them onto the cooling racks. The two of them moved swiftly, but it wasn't stressful, and their work took on an easy cadence. As soon as the cookies were just cool enough, he outlined each with icing using the piping tip and then he did the flooding. She added the details, and when she finished a tray, he moved it to dry under the fan. They hardly spoke a word, but their silence wasn't awkward. To the contrary, the space between them hummed in an energetic way, like they were keenly connected.

Finally, hallelujah, hurray! They arranged the cookies in layers in the boxes and loaded them into the van. To be extra safe, and without requiring any prior discussion, neither of them carried out more than a single box at one time.

Standing near the back door, she took off her hair net, while he removed his cap. She changed out of her clogs and into her flats; he put his Santa suit back on.

She would miss the sight of him in his jeans and T-shirt, but it was for the best.

As she closed the back door behind them, she noticed

the mess they had made on the counter. She would clean it up tomorrow. There, she had a project to distract her and an excuse to keep their coffee date—no, their coffee *meeting*—short.

She turned her key in the lock just as he startled her with upbeat Santa-excitement in his voice. "Wait, what about your dress? Won't you need it for the gala?"

"I was planning to change here after we deliver, but I guess you're right—it's probably better to take it along so I can change in the country club ladies' room." She had not been thinking about the gala at all, she was focused on fulfilling the late orders. But returning to the bakery would take extra time, and time was still not on her side.

She ran back in, straight to her office, grabbed the tote with her shoes and makeup and threw it over her shoulder, took the hanger with her dress down from the hook on the door. When she came out carrying it over her forearm, James' eyes shot right to it.

She wondered what he was thinking. Although, if his thoughts were anything like the images that began to run through her own mind of the two of them on some romantic date—and, mainly, what would happen after—it would be best not to ask him.

They jumped into her van, closed their doors, drove north toward Sunset Beach and Huntington Harbour. She pulled up in front of Guy's and Evelyn's house to drop James off with the cookies for their party.

"I have more deliveries nearby," she told him as he undid his seatbelt. In addition to the Chakrabartis and the Bensons, the Golds, the Flanders, and a few of the other impacted clients also lived close by. "So, Santa," she said, turning to face him. "I'll swing by to pick you up as soon as I'm done with those drop-offs in—give or take—an hour."

"Sounds like a plan, milady. Good luck with your mission." He leaned over and kissed her fast on the cheek goodbye. "Sorry!" he said instantly. "I didn't mean... I don't know why I did that... I heard what you said before. Sorry, just, sorry."

As he shut the door shaking his head and looking all flustered, she assured him it was okay, that she wasn't angry. She understood the impulsive kiss had been unconscious. But what shocked her even more than his spontaneity, she realized as she touched the side of her face where his lips had grazed, was how utterly natural it felt.

Chapter 11
weird instinct

WTF, *man?* James could not articulate why he kissed her goodbye, except for being driven by pure instinct and clearly not rational thought.

Instinct, okay, yes. He would go with that because it was his best guess. And now remembering that kiss, not to mention the ones that came before, was going to torture him, especially the scent of her skin and how soft it looked from his vantage point, where he was able to see the curve of her neck.

She had seemed shocked but not immediately. It took a moment, almost like surprise hit her after the realization kicked in. So that might be a positive sign, that viscerally in that split second, him kissing her goodbye as if he always hopped out of her van hadn't been so outlandish.

Mentally, he shifted gears as he closed the passenger door and went around to the back to get the cookies. Those three large green boxes, he carried them up Guy's walk as if they were a delicate treasure. Along the curving paving stones past carefully landscaped beds of succulents and wild grasses, he walked cautiously to the modern glass and wood house, peering around the corner of the boxes. The mellow smell of sage in the air reminded him to inhale a deep breath and chill out. Because, heaven forbid he trip.

"Thank goodness you're here," Guy said as he met James at the front door. "The kids are getting restless." Guy relieved him of the boxes, and suggested he go around the back. "The patio doors are open, and there's a large double-sided fireplace that's part indoors and part out. I was thinking you could sit in there until my wife brings the kids down to the den in a few minutes. You know, make it look like you just came down the chimney."

"Great idea," James said, his inner-Santa smile returning.

He followed Guy's directions around to the back gate and—holy cow, the man wasn't exaggerating. The fireplace was practically the size of James' whole apartment.

He crouched inside to wait and even though it was an inopportune moment, his thoughts turned to Anna. Specifically they turned to the dress he had seen earlier in her office that she had hung on the back hook in the van. Instead of her going to her gala all alone, he fantasized about taking her, like they were on an elegant Christmas Eve date.

Why either of them would agree to that after all the baggage previously discussed, he wasn't sure, but a man could dream. Including about unzipping the back of that sexy dress after the gala when they got home.

The rumbling of many young, eager feet on the floor overhead and at the top of the stairs told him the kids were clamoring to make their way down, so he set his Anna-in-a-long-red- gown musing aside.

For the second time today, playing Santa with the children gave him more to think about than loss. The kids were precocious and funny, still young and, mostly, unjaded; the whole idea of Santa Claus hadn't yet lost its luster.

While he visited with them and asked about their Christmas lists and plans, Evelyn took a ton of photos with her phone. During a brief lull in activity, she turned the screen and scrolled through the images so he could see them. It was clear from all the smiles and laughter and, in the background, the empty cookie boxes on the table that, even without the bounce house, the kids were having a great time.

When he said goodbye an hour later, he told the kids Santa had to leave for a special last-minute assignment—to help the lady who baked the cookies deliver to other Christmas parties.

The kids' antics and good humor buoyed him as did the sight of Anna again, and he decided to take a risk. When he climbed into her van, he quickly leaned in and gave her smiling face another quick peck. This time, what he said was more calculated: "Hi Honey, I'm home."

The sound of her laughter and that flash of a grin, they were the best Christmas gifts he had received in a very long while. Suddenly, though, he felt sheepish about joking like that. It was one thing to imagine in your own head, another to find out how it would actually land. "Was that any less weird?" he asked as he settled into the passenger seat, pulled the seatbelt across his body, and clicked it in.

"A little? Not really," she clarified, shooting him a...teasing?...glance while shifting into gear.

They soon turned back onto PCH and headed south to Balboa Island and the peninsula and then further on to Laguna Beach, where homes perched on bluffs overlooked the ocean.

By Ninth Avenue, they passed the entrance down to Thousand Steps Beach, and he recalled having been there before—the cliffs, the tide pools, the rocks—but not in ages. He decided then and there to check it out again while he was in town. Maybe she would agree to go with him. They could look out at the water, explore the sea cave at low tide.

And then he exhaled a deep breath as they drove onward. The energy settled; they had a few moments of calm. In the quiet, he remembered the ornament. "Hey," he started, looking at her in profile. "We were busy with the baking, but I wanted to ask you, "How do you know Lucy Washingtonn?"

Again, James saw that stunned look in her widened eyes, along with a weak—or was it sad?—lip movement that sort of but not really formed a smile, and he realized it was usually better not to just blurt out questions without offering context.

"It's just, I saw the ornament on your desk, and I remembered seeing the same one in Dr. Washingtonn's office at the hospital. She was our...my...therapist there, and she told me her granddaughter made it, that they baked Christmas cookies together. Maybe it's a coincidence you have the same ornament—but since she said it was hand-made...I was wondering if she's somehow..."

He was going to say, 'related,' but Anna cut in. "My mother." She slowed the car to enlarge the street map on her phone and maybe also to regroup because she seemed dumbfounded. He tried to imagine her expression if she weren't trying to focus on the road and navigate under pressure. He should have waited to ask. His timing obviously still needed work.

"Really. Huh. Wow. That's unbelievable," he blabbered, trying to scramble back to their easy, chill vibe. "I mean, what are the chances, what a small world. When I said earlier the hospital staff were amazing, she's one of the main people I was talking about. In fact, earlier today I finally went by her old office, and it didn't look like she used it anymore. Where is she now, what's she doing? Did she retire from the job?"

He finally stopped his motor mouth from running so she could answer his questions.

Only she wasn't. In fact, now she wasn't just slowing down but pulling over.

He looked at her and, whatever the specific reason, he promptly felt like an oaf. Because the look on her face told him her answer was going to be bad news.

"She's unfortunately no longer with us." Her voice was low, its cadence slow, and man, he felt so stupid with his questions that made assumptions. "I wish I could say she was happily retired, golfing, still volunteering, and baking with Carli and me every Christmas. But she's not. She suffered an aneurysm about four and a half years ago."

She didn't tear up, but her eyes suddenly looked so forlorn that he wished they weren't in the car so he could properly hug her.

"Oh, no, Anna. I'm sorry. She was so caring. And vivacious and wise."

"Yes, she was all those things. I was grateful it happened quickly and that she didn't suffer, but it was such a shock. And a few months after she died, Blake told me he wanted the divorce. I had no idea how I would get through that time without her." She glanced at the time on the dashboard clock, her jaw tensed, and slowly she pulled away from the shoulder.

Soon, as they approached Vista del Mar, she put the left blinker on. "I'm just so sorry," he said again, at a loss for more words as he processed how alone she must have felt. And then he thought of a way he might, even now, be able to offer comfort. "Can I share a Dr. Washingtonn story?"

"Please." More than her saying that word, her small smile—this time it was a smile in earnest—told him her answer was yes.

"When we were there, at the hospital, with my son on Christmas Eve, Santa came to his room to visit. The guy was really great with him, and once he left and Claire was reading Noah a story, I wandered down to Dr....to your mother's office." As he spoke, in the background his brain chewed on this new fact, that he was sitting here in a car with a woman he just met, who also happened to be Dr. Washingtonn's daughter.

"She asked how the Santa visit was, and I told her how great the guy handled Noah, and that if circumstances were different, how playing Santa for kids stuck in a hospital at Christmas would be a great gig. A way for them to have a good—I mean, a semi-normal—time. She nodded in that therapist way of hers and asked me point-blank, 'Why don't you do it?'"

As the car rounded a hilly curve to the left, he caught a glimpse of Anna's lovely neck. Quickly, he looked away and focused instead on the landscape, so he didn't lose his train of thought. "I must have looked confused, so your mom clarified, 'Play Santa next year. We need to fatten you up, though,' she said, 'I'll bring in some of the cookies I made with my family last night, so come by again tomorrow.'"

He hoped his sharing the memory wasn't upsetting, but

to his relief Anna laughed softly. "I remember that Christmas Eve," she said. "Blake took Ben to the movies, and Carli and I were at her house. We made snowballs and chocolate chip."

"My experience of your mother was that she was gentle but firm, and I could tell she was not going to let me off the hook. 'Really James. I think we're onto something. Consider volunteering with kids at some point. You'll know when it's time. Will you promise me you'll do it?' I said I would but for the life of me, I couldn't imagine when."

"Until now," Anna said.

"Until now," he repeated. "How long did she work at the hospital?"

"Many years—I don't know exactly how many, to tell you the truth. Technically she wasn't employed by the hospital—she had her own private therapy practice—but she was a loyal volunteer."

"I didn't realize that. It seemed like whenever I went to her office, whenever I needed to talk or, more often, just needed to get away from everything, her door was open; she was always there."

"That's kind of how she was as a mother, and a grandmother—really caring and...always there."

"Is that why you bake the cookies now, why you donate every year?"

"Mm-hm," she said, glancing at him before turning back to watch the road. "She's the reason why. After she died, I wanted to do something to honor her but I wasn't sure what, and then as soon as I started baking professionally it hit me. Loads of Christmas cookies to share with all those kids and parents? She would have loved the idea."

And maybe also the fact that the day I finally put on that Santa costume, we met.

And that was the extent to which he had time to consider fate or coincidence, karma or the universe's strange ways of working, because they were approaching the next address.

She stopped the car at the foot of the driveway, and they both hurried out of the car. He barely heard his phone buzz from its spot in the passenger side cupholder as he slammed the door, ignoring it. Anna took three boxes from the back of the van, and carefully he picked up the fourth.

James playing Santa at Guy's home had inspired the two of them, and as soon as she picked him up after his second gig of the day, they had quickly agreed: At each client's door, he would slip into his Santa role. He apologized to all the parents, explained the reason for the delay, took quick photos with their kids. Meanwhile, Anna would wish them a merry Christmas and wave goodbye as she rushed back to the driver's side of her van. He would jog to catch up and hop in fast and then off they would drive to the next customer's house.

They repeated the process at every door, including this one, where she was ringing the bell of a brick and stone mid-century ranch.

More than once he was star-struck when he recognized the personalities who greeted them. It was good that she usually started off by introducing him: "This is my friend Santa," she would say as she handed them their cookie boxes, since it gave him a few seconds to collect himself. He loved seeing her interact with her customers. She behaved how he suspected she most often did when stress and worry about disappointing others wasn't weighing her down: genuine, funny, self-deprecating.

As they traveled through the neighborhoods to drop off each order, they turned up the radio and sang along to

Christmas carols. And because Hanukkah started two days ago, they also sang the dreidel song and the one about the latkes. He was a terrible singer, and although Anna was better but still not fantastic, he couldn't help but notice, somehow their voices harmonized. It wasn't only that he heard the sound. With each note, his body thrummed; the resonance, *their* resonance, he felt it.

Chapter 12
one stop

S inging off-key, humming now and then when they both forgot the words, groaning at dumb jokes— underneath his sedate manner, James was quite funny. Riding in the van together felt like being cocooned inside their own Christmas snow-globe bubble. Or rather sand globe, since there wasn't much snow in this part of California. And the connection to her mother? Maybe if Anna had been less stressed out today, she might have thought to ask him if he had met her mom when he first said he had spent time at the hospital with his son. With how the afternoon had played out after he crashed into her this morning, though, just about everything else but baking new cookies and willing the power to come back on had totally slipped her mind.

When the last drop-off was done in Laguna Hills, she pulled over around the corner from the client's house, leaned back against the headrest, breathed a deep sigh of relief, and turned in his direction. "We made it. I can't believe we're done." She shook her head at how the carefully scheduled day had jumped the rails and at the coincidence of their connection.

Then the dashboard clock ticked, and drew her awareness. The gala. She didn't have time to think much about kismet. "You said you live in Irvine, right?"

"Right."

"Okay, so I'll drop you off and head to the club and that should give me just enough time to change. Actually, would you mind driving to your place so I can text the kids? It's been a while since they checked in."

It was strange that Carli hadn't texted a photo of the concert or her new watch, even though she knew Anna wasn't happy about it. That was one thing to appreciate in a teenager, that Carli still felt connected to her no matter what transpired, and the mood swings meant her bursts of anger didn't last.

"I would love to play chauffeur, milady; allow me to commandeer the sleigh."

James opened the passenger door to get out so they could switch. She did the same while shaking her head and chuckling at his goofy humor. But there was more to it, and the feeling of tension and tightness eased somewhere inside her chest. It wasn't only that he took over driving; it was the enjoyment of his company, his humor, of the feeling she had someone to turn to—not any someone, but James—to ask a favor of and have the answer not be argumentative or resentful but a glad-to-help and interested *yes*.

He put his address into her GPS because he said he didn't want to risk getting lost again. Which reminded her of this morning and how him losing his way coupled with the wind—and his promise to her mother—had led to their chance encounter. She could only shake her head.

The GPS route took them through the winding streets

of another hilltop Laguna neighborhood with amazing displays of Christmas lights. He drove carefully, as fast as the speed signs allowed, and they ogled the yards as they whizzed by.

While they snaked down the winding road, his eyes remained forward to focus on the street ahead, but he and Anna kept right on talking.

"Do you have a favorite Christmas tradition?" he wanted to know. "I mean, besides baking cookies with your mom," he added.

"Aside from baking with her in the past and now delivering to the customers, tradition? Hm, I'm not sure. That implies repetition, and the way things have worked out since I opened the bakery, the kids have spent it with their dad. But a couple of years ago, Blake had to change travel dates, so that Christmas Eve they stayed with me. After the cookie deliveries, I took them to Crystal Cove in the evening to see the Christmas tree. They loved that."

At the memory, she closed her eyes to hold onto it longer, felt the smile soften her face. "That was a fun night," she said. "Not only for the kids; I loved it too."

"If you didn't have the gala—and if the winds weren't so unpredictable today—I would suggest we go." He turned toward her for a quick second. "Uh, sorry," he said before she could respond. "I don't mean to be presumptuous. I know it's not the same going without your kids, or that you'd want to go with me, but it could be a nice way to wind down a really, *really* strange day."

Although she knew the time, had been aware of it dwindling all day, she found herself shooting another look at the dashboard clock. The gala was starting in less than an hour. Otherwise, yes, it would be nice to go to Crystal Cove, sit on a piece of driftwood and watch the ocean. She would take photos to send the kids of the cottages with their offbeat decorations and of course the big Christmas tree.

And also, it would be nice to sit on a driftwood log and look out at the ocean beside James. She imagined the warmth of his body next to hers, how if they sat close enough, their shoulders and thighs would touch.

Although their delivery drive had been frenzied, and the familiarity of that surprise goodbye peck on the cheek outside Guy's was way weird, she had to admit he was a wonderful companion. The way he joked and sang adorably but badly, not that she was any better, how he helped her so the baking and deliveries would go faster, how at each house he delighted everyone by playing Santa. But most of all, him just being there.

That thought sunk in as he turned another corner and approached the on-ramp to the freeway. Their time together was winding down. She might have been right to push him away earlier; she had to concentrate, not neck like a horny teenager in the bakery's back room. And everything she had told him was true. She wasn't ready to get involved because, well, for the many reasons they already covered.

But then she turned to watch him in profile, and seeing the wrinkles at the corner of his eye from that laugh she already loved to hear was having a calming effect. Also, it seemed like her mother had liked him if she encouraged him to play Santa. What would be the harm in hanging out, in being friends, in doing some activities together?

Anna pictured him coming over for dinner sometime. The kids would like his sense of humor, and they would appreciate that he had known their grandmother. Maybe they could barbeque in her condo's small back courtyard and invite him to join in.

Why couldn't Anna see him again?

Why not tonight?

* * *

"It would be nice to go to the beach, I agree. But James, about the gala, what if... Would you like to come with me?"

For a quick second, he took his eyes off the road, turned to look at her with surprise or...his expression was closer to shock, and then immediately he swallowed, looked like he was thinking.

"I would love to accompany you to the gala, Anna." The humor had left his voice when he spoke, and its pitch now sounded lower. "But," he added, clearing his throat, "I can tell from your dress it's a black-tie event, and I don't have a tux."

His earnestness was touching and sweet, and given the situation, it also made her giggle. She narrowed her eyes and pursed her lips to give him a feigned assessing look. "For this occasion, your current attire strikes me as *the* perfect fit."

He relaxed and those wrinkles she had been watching by his eye contracted when he grinned. "You have a point there, and in that case I'd love to accompany you, milady. Since my place is on the way, you're welcome to come in and change. Although the country club probably has infinitely more luxurious facilities."

He drove them to his apartment complex, and she followed him up the stairs of his building while he conscientiously carried her dress. He unlocked the door and waited for her to enter.

It was hard to imagine the warm, playful James she knew from today living here. It didn't feel at all like him.

Two words that sprang to mind were, *nondescript* and *austere*.

"It's nothing special but," he shrugged, "I'm hardly ever here."

There was a small square of tile by the entry, and a dim light hung from the ceiling in the living room, which held a beat-up sofa, a table, and several stacks of cardboard moving boxes.

She could relate. It had also taken her and the kids a while to unpack after they moved from the Balboa house to her condo. But something didn't sit right; a bad feeling rose in her stomach. That article about him taking the hospital job, it was at least six months ago. What she was looking at wasn't a few last things not yet put away; the piles of boxes looked like they were just waiting for movers to carry out.

He looked around as if seeing the space anew, based on what must have been her visible reaction. "It's definitely a bachelor pad," he explained. "I haven't had time to settle in." His gaze dropped, then rose again but he didn't meet her eyes. "The bathroom's this way. Here, I'll hang your dress."

"I understand, no need to explain." She opened her tote to take out her makeup bag and set it on the bathroom counter. The small space was tidy, his few things neatly organized, although seeing the single toothbrush in the holder with four spaces gave her a stab of sadness.

"I'll just be a few minutes," she told him. She closed the door and got to work, letting down her hair and shaking flour dust out of it into the sink. A few swipes with her hair-brush to add volume and she gathered it again, twisting it into an updo high on the back of her head. Strategically placed bobby pins held it up, and she pulled a few wavy strands down to frame her face.

On to makeup next—powder with a subtle sparkle, blush, eyeshadow, mascara, and her favorite, special occasion lipstick—and then she checked the time, which now was really running out. Quickly, she undressed, rolled up her clothes and stuffed them in her tote, and then she put on the dress.

It had been a lucky find at the discount outlet of a high-end retailer during an end-of-season sale, and she hadn't had occasion to wear it yet. As she put it on, the silky red material felt luxurious against her skin. It sat smoothly on her hips and hugged her curves without making her feel stuffed into a sausage skin.

The reflection in the vanity mirror looked back at her, feminine and... attractive? Good lord, since she had felt like that, how long had it been? A shiver of excitement at seeing James' response when she emerged prompted her to rub her arms, where goosebumps had quickly risen. But then reality returned, along with that familiar feeling of expecting to be let down.

That uneasy sensation in her belly was more than butterflies about the gala. It lacked that sense of hopeful anticipation, and as it swirled and took up more space, it began to feel like dismay. The phone calls he ignored today, the lack of furniture and pictures in the apartment, the pain over his son and a failed marriage—it all added up. James was lost. Not only literally this morning, making a wrong turn down the alley on his way to the hospital, but figuratively as well. His time here—she just knew it intuitively—it would be temporary.

One stop on the line, not a place to stay. And emotionally, she knew this too: He would withdraw and pull away.

It had been stupid of her in the car to think there could be anything, even friendship, between them. After all, they only met a few hours ago and only because he bumped into her. It wasn't like some rom-com meet cute or like a dating app mutual swipe in the same direction. He had thrown her whole day into a tizzy. He had almost cost her her loyal customers and, if she hadn't finished re-baking and delivering in the nick of time, he could have disqualified her from the Angels' competition.

Was she that desperate for a man's attention? That hard up that she could, even for a brief time, lose sight of her vision, her principles, her goals?

Don't answer that.

When she came out of the bathroom, he was sitting on the couch looking at his phone, and she pushed her shoulders back to fortify her resolve. "Thank you for the help today, but on second thought, I've decided to attend the gala alone."

He blinked a few times, and his eyes changed shape as he processed. "Anna, what? What happened? Why?"

She gestured around his apartment as she walked toward the front door. "It was nice. Today. So nice, if I'm honest."

Too nice. Too good to be true.

"And it got me thinking about how wonderful it might be—"

"I know, Anna," he interrupted, "it's been the same for me. But I don't understand. In the car"—he pointed in the direction of the parking lot—"I mean, you *just* invited me to join you. Why the sudden change of heart?"

"You're not in any position to start a new...anything. This"—she swept her arm to indicate his living space—"it's temporary. It's obvious you're just passing through. I may be the one leaving right now for the gala but *you're* the one who will run away."

* * *

Again. James waited for her to add that word. She didn't, but only because she didn't know his itinerant history. If she did, she definitely would have said it. And also because she was out his front door too fast to say anything. And also, also, he didn't chase her. Because he didn't want to make her late. And also, also, also, what could he say?

He never should have agreed to her invitation. What had he been thinking? She would drop off the broken cookie crumbles tomorrow morning, have a quick cup of coffee, and that would be that. No awkward just-friends friendship, no uncomfortable beach outings that felt too much like dates, neither of them risking a broken heart again.

Right?

He sat on his piece-of-shit couch, looked around, and took it all in—not only the bare apartment but his entire situation—from the point of view of a stranger.

No, not a stranger, but Anna.

Because no matter what he told himself, he cared what this woman thought, and in the short time they had shared each other's company today, she had unknowingly done something he hadn't thought possible: She had gotten him to consider his future.

He took note of the emptiness, the lack, the space devoid of photos and meaningful knickknacks, the absence of a single Christmas memento or decoration.

The optics, he had to say, were not on his side where Anna's observation was concerned. Because this apartment? She was right, although she hadn't said it in precisely so many words: It was the antithesis of a home.

His phone rang again and when he flipped it open, he saw the headhunter was calling him back.

"Hello and Merry Christmas to you, too," he said. "No, I haven't listened to my voicemail, but I take it you have news?" He tried to sound upbeat at that last part.

"I do. So the Portland conference center job we talked about briefly, I just got off a call with the HR director, and they want you to join their team as executive chef. The pay would be twenty percent more than what you're earning now, and they added a generous signing bonus as incentive. You'll get a housing subsidy for the rentals on the premises. She said there happens to be one opening up in a few weeks with a view down to the river."

"Wow, that is great news," was all he managed to say. He hoped it didn't sound as flat, as devoid of feeling, as it did to his own ear.

It was great news, though. He could give notice at the hospital tomorrow and stay for another couple of months until they found a replacement. He had been there barely six months; one of the previous candidates who had applied when he did might still be available so he wouldn't leave his boss hanging.

The pay would be better in Portland, and a pad with a view of the Willamette was hard to argue with.

No southern California traffic, no unpredictable winds causing problems.

No Anna.

"You don't sound super-excited. Is it the money? Because I might be able to push them higher."

"No, it's not that. The money is fine." It wasn't like his monk-like existence cost very much.

"Then what is it? To find you the right position in the right place, I have to know what you're thinking."

Today, this weird unexpected day, had caused an internal

shift. It was a combination of things: the delivery drive, seeing so many houses lit by celebration and laughter from within, Austin's bittersweet wisdom echoing in his mind.

And the most impactful, how he had felt all day with Anna beside him.

He wasn't completely daft; he knew he couldn't say no to a good gig for the hope of something developing between them. After what she had said a few moments ago, she was probably done with him altogether, and he really couldn't blame her.

But he could make another attempt, and he could also stay here for other reasons. Reasons like, that he enjoyed his current job a lot, and it was important to him to help provide nourishment for an organization that did good work. Also, driving the circuitous route this afternoon reminded him of how much there was to rediscover about this area.

Familiarity and novelty, both now felt important.

And last but hardly least, because it was time to prove, not to anyone else but himself, that he no longer needed to keep moving. No place on Earth would take away the loss or sadness, and that would never change. So he could start fresh right here—or rather, continue on, figure out how to integrate the past.

Like Austin wished for his parents, Noah wouldn't want James to, as he would have put it in little-boy terms, be sad. He would want James to laugh, to live his life.

Damn it, his chest still ached, and it probably always would. But living and occasional laughter in itself would be a way to honor him, to put to good use the time he would never have.

Time that could also include playing Santa at the

hospital again next year and maybe—maybe—help Anna bake and deliver her cookies.

So he finally grew a pair.

"I really appreciate the opportunity—it sounds amazing, especially with the river view," he said. "But I like it here—both the job and the place—and I've decided, I'm not going to take a new position. I don't want to move again."

"Why don't you think about it over Christmas, and I'll call you back on the twenty-sixth or twenty-seventh. It's a great opportunity, and you're approaching your six-month mark. I'm sure you're eager to move on to something else. So sleep on it. Don't make a decision yet."

"That's okay, I'm positive. I'm tired of feeling lost and disoriented in each new location. It's time to think about how to put down some roots. So thank you for all your hard work on my behalf, but I no longer need your services."

They hung up, and he went into the bathroom to comb his hair and shave. The scent of Anna's perfume still lingering in the air made him certain about his new plan.

He would drive to the club to talk to her. To let her know he was serious, to show her he was *not* a runner. And if she was too busy to talk with him at the gala, at least he could see her win the competition.

Because he knew she would.

But before he left the apartment, he had one thing more to do: call Claire. He wanted to get it over with, tell her he would like to drop the Christmas call, check in with each other every once in a while, whenever it felt right. He wouldn't say this, but knowing they would talk had become a bleak routine, and waiting for it always gave him a sick feeling in his stomach.

Not speaking to her on Christmas wouldn't erase or minimize the mutual loss, but it might help him—help both of them—think about the holiday differently going forward. Instead of only holding sadness, maybe there could also be room to create new memories, possibly even celebrate in some small and meaningful ways.

He got to the club right as the heavy wooden doors were closing, but the two attendants waved him in without asking for his name or to see an invitation. *Thank you, Santa attire.* That was one obstacle out of the way, that he didn't have to say he was Anna's or Guy's guest, which was his immediately-conceived if slightly not-transparent backup plan.

The sign on the easel told him the O.C. Christmas Angels' event was being held in the banquet hall, straight ahead. The huge room was decked in full Christmas regalia. Evergreen and holly boughs with red bows and gold ornaments encircled the walls, and in the back not far from where he entered, stood a tall, impressively tall, and beautifully decorated tree.

The largest chandelier he ever saw hung from the center of the ceiling diffusing soft light around the space, while tall candles on each of the round dining tables cast a romantic glow. The only strong lighting was focused on the raised dais, where Anna was seated along with the other finalists.

She looked gorgeous up there because she just was, and her hair, her dress, her eyes, the sparkle of her smile and her personality, they all contributed to her bearing. It was hard not to stand there and gawk as she chatted with the woman beside her, but he stopped himself from staring because he needed to better plot his game plan.

He could not let her see him because she might get distracted or be angry that he was there, which—why was he only realizing this now?—was a distinct possibility. What seemed like the only right thing to do when he was in his apartment now struck him as a bad idea. To thrust himself into her life, to show up here after she told him in no uncertain terms she wanted to attend alone?

For the second or third or fourth time today—he lost count—he had to ask himself, *WTF?* Because apparently crashing into her this morning had scrambled his brain.

Tonight was about her and the competition, and he would not do anything to jeopardize it. He would leave as soon as the winner was announced, well before she came down to the main floor. It would be better to get out of dodge right now and not wait, but—he glanced down at his outfit—he was not exactly dressed inconspicuously. If he left now, just as things were about to start, she would most likely see him. So he stayed off to the side and way in the back and because his pulse now pounded from anxiety and second-guessing, he did what instinct propelled him to do: He made a quick run for it and hid behind the tree.

Chapter 13
gift horse

Although Anna couldn't see very much with the lights shining down on the makeshift stage, she could hear the audience's chatter begin to hush. Off to the side, Guy climbed the short staircase onto the platform and started to welcome everyone. In his tuxedo, red bowtie, and a matching cummerbund, he looked dapper and, thankfully, a lot calmer than at the bakery earlier today.

He said a few words about the history of the group and introduced the angel investors, who were seated amid the audience. Then he asked the finalists to share a little about themselves, their business, their connection to Orange County.

When it was her turn, Anna stood and explained how baking most of her life with her late mother had inspired her to start her business. She went on to add how single-parenting and wanting to provide opportunities for her children inspired her vision of opening a second location.

She kept it high-level. She would never publicly share her fantasy about Carli or Ben one day taking over. If that got onto social media and the kids saw it, Ben would be fine but Carli would go ballistic. Anna could hear the accusation, "Why are you trying to control my future!?" *Stupid bakery.*

The rest of the finalists introduced themselves, and then Guy explained more about the Angels' competition.

"As you may know, we have a longstanding annual Christmas tradition. Earlier in the year, we solicit proposals from businesses seeking growth capital, and then we spend an intense few months reviewing them and selecting the top contenders—business leaders from the community who we admire and want to support. This means for one of the five individuals seated before you on the stage, whose name I'll announce in a moment, the O.C. Christmas Angels will give that lucky person a boost so they can fund their venture."

Guy's phrasing struck her as kind of funny, and she wasn't the only one. Laughter from the audience rippled softly around the room. Anna mentally waved away the image of the marble counter and multiple front glass cases she envisioned for her second shop. There were four other people sitting beside her, so she was hardly a shoo-in for angel investment. Quite the opposite actually; if you did the math, she only had a pretty lousy one-in-five chance of winning.

"Seriously," Guy was saying, "We've brought these five finalists here tonight, Christmas Eve, because we've been observing their young businesses over the past few months. Since reviewing their proposals and reading about their plans, we've done a lot of research. We've frequented their establishments, sent in secret shoppers, ordered from their websites, studied their financials and management practices, thoroughly done our diligence. Among the many businesses that submitted proposals, we winnowed it down to the most promising, the five of you."

Now he angled his body away from the audience and more toward them. "Only one of you will get our financial backing this year. Our support comes with a fixed dollar amount, in exchange for a percentage of ownership, and we'll work with you to further refine your business plans to help you achieve your goals."

Her hands had been folded in her lap, and she pressed them tighter in hopeful anticipation. Again and despite trying hard to control them, visions of her second store advanced like a slideshow in her mind.

"And the winner is..."

Anna's Bakery of Cookies—that's me!

* * *

A surge of pride and excitement rose in her body. Her heart pounded in her ears, and her palms broke out in sweat while her mouth went sandpaper dry.

Guy was talking about her proposal, explaining how Anna's clear, compelling vision and steadfast dedication had convinced the committee, and that the Angels had hopeful plans.

"One of the most rewarding things about this event is the chance to share the potential *we* see that the entrepreneurs themselves often miss since we have distance and," he angled his body further in Anna's direction, "because it's your baby, your business, to be frank, sometimes you don't."

The crowd laughed again; many guests nodded their heads in agreement. Guy shifted his weight and took a breath to continue. "Anna, we're so impressed with the business you've built with your talent as a cookie baker, your entrepreneurial acumen, and also the generous way you give back to the community. Your children's hospital Christmas cookie donation each year has become legend."

She mouthed thank you, brought her hands together by her chest in prayer pose as he went on. "And what I personally observed today, when you were faced with a difficult situation, showed the depth of your dedication. We see *so* much potential for Anna's Bakery of Cookies. Your proposal outlined your plans for a second location, but we envision a lot more than that—along with a lot of dough."

The cheerful audience mock-groaned. Baking puns, she knew from her own past attempts, rarely went well. "I know, I know. My wife warned me not to use that one," Guy said. Laughter now, including Anna's own.

"But let me get back to business: We see additional bakery locations in Orange County in the next three years, grow it into a chain, create a franchise model, perhaps expand outside California." Guy's words sped up with his palpable excitement.

"That's incredible," Anna said. It was good she was seated because her crossed legs started to wobble. She uncrossed them and planted both feet firmly on the platform to feel more grounded while Guy kept on talking.

"We did some preliminary research on extruders, icing machines, and streamlining recipes so they're suitable for pre-made mixes. We'll be able to scale you up, ship everywhere, put frozen dough in grocery store coolers, generate *enormous* profit."

Wait....Frozen dough? Extruders? Pre-made mixes and icing machines?

That was so not what her bakery was about. And then a couple of memories surfaced: Anna as a little girl standing on a step-stool next to her mother at their kitchen counter, bringing the big bowl to her chest to stir, her mom's patience and warm smile as Anna tried to carefully ice the cookies that had cooled. She pictured the bakery, her mother's handwritten recipes sealed in plastic for longevity and clipped to the shelves, the expressions on her customers' faces when they looked at the finished products stacked in the small glass case.

Disappointment fell like a weight inside her chest. It was sounding like she and the Angels might not be on the same page.

"Anna, congratulations. You've already built a great foundation. With our investment, we believe you'll have a *real* winner on your hands."

Her foundation of a business had gotten her and the kids through the darkest time of her, of their, life. She had built it from scratch with nothing other than a crazy idea, determination to create security for her family, and a whole lot of sweat equity. The bakery did not turn an enormous profit, but it was enough to take care of the three of them and not have to rely on Blake for anything. In her mind, in her heart, it was already a winner.

And the recipes the Angels wanted to streamline into a shippable mix and non-perishable supermarket dough?

"Really incredible," she repeated to buy herself a moment to figure out what she needed to say, as much as it pained her.

Her knees started to feel less wobbly. Slowly she stood up and inhaled deeply, blew the breath out her mouth, tried not to puff her cheeks as she decided where to start.

"Guy, members of the committee, working with you would be an unbelievable opportunity, and I'm so grateful to all of you for offering me this chance. I made a brand commitment when I started the bakery, in other words, a promise to my customers. That the cookies I baked would be made and decorated by hand, with high-quality, local ingredients from genuine family recipes.

"My mother, who sadly is no longer with us, taught me how to bake many of those cookies since I was a child; they're an important connection to her memory. The recipes are significant; they represent family and tradition. They mean keeping experiences alive that I hold dear. All the time, but especially at Christmas."

Except for some annoying rustling in the back by the big tree, you could hear a shortbread crumb drop, the room was so quiet.

"Streamlining them," she went on, "to optimize for commodification or a higher profit margin would be anathema to the bakery's mission. And if I project two or three years ahead based on your vision, I can see that I would be faced with an impossible choice: to be a baker *or* a back-office business person because it would be too large an operation for me to do both. With all due respect, the type of baking you're talking about would have a completely different character. I didn't start the company to be a cookie machine operator—or a chief financial officer."

"Surely you understand that without these changes, you won't be able to scale successfully," Guy said. "So what are you telling us, Anna?"

"What I'm saying is, I suppose the answer to your question about scale depends on one's definition of success. I do believe there are ways to grow sustainably and profitably, that don't change the essence of what my customers expect and of what I love about running my business. What I'm saying is, respectfully, I'm afraid I have no choice but to decline the Angel's generous offer."

* * *

When Anna took a new seat at one of the many tables on the main floor as the dinner service began, the woman next to her touched her forearm. "Good for you," she whispered while the others nearby smiled uncomfortably or averted their eyes.

Wait staff in black pants, white shirts, and red Santa hats brought carefully arranged plates of food that smelled scrumptious. *If* you felt hungry, which she didn't.

What she did feel was a quick prick of second-guessing followed by the calmness of certainty. Declining the Angels' offer was the right thing. She would add a second location with—okay, maybe not two or three but one—yes, one marble island, and then open additional shops slowly, as time and money allowed.

She would be patient. Not to rush resting dough, wasn't that a lesson any baker worth her salt knew? It would be a lot of work since slow wasn't the easiest strategy. There had been a few times since she opened, with simultaneous large orders to fill and a looming delivery deadline, when she had wished for a little assist from production equipment. But those moments were the rare exceptions, not the rule.

She could do it. The prospect of hard work didn't scare her.

Neither did the possibility that, no matter how many hours she put in, how much of herself she invested, it still might not go as planned. That lesson she had learned from her ruined marriage, and it also applied to the bakery. In fact, it presented itself again when James crashed into her this morning. And as he helped her this afternoon, he voiced it. *Life comes with no guarantees.*

She tried to flick the image of him away. She would

keep her gaze leveled on the horizon; she would stay focused on her business and its future.

Focused.

The immediate past, how nice it had felt to work side by side baking? To spend the day together? To kiss him? She could think—and maybe indulge in a brief, very brief, cry—about that later.

She might also cry because she wished she could share the story of today with her mother, who would have been so proud of how Anna stood up for her convictions and also—so much for focusing—tickled no end at how she and James met.

But instead of crying, Anna watched Guy come striding over.

She prepared to explain again, but he began to speak first. "Anna, you're the only business owner in the history of the O.C. Christmas Angels to reject us, and I have to say it impressed us even more."

"It wasn't easy," she said, grimacing sheepishly and shaking her head to underscore that the decision to turn them down had been hard. "I meant what I said—I'm very grateful to have been chosen."

"We appreciated your candor and how you addressed the whole group rather than tell us privately later on. You set a great example. Not every business is a fit for us, and it's good for the other owners here tonight to hear from a fellow entrepreneur some of the reasons why."

"Okay, good, I'm glad I didn't offend."

"To the contrary. We'd actually like you to join our group—as a consulting associate. Typically, members bring significant funds to invest, but we don't want money from you because you should be putting it into your own busi-ness. We're confident we would benefit from your insight, and we know other owners would too, so what do you say—will you be part of the O.C. Christmas Angels?"

She did not have to think about that for any amount of time. "When's your next meeting?"

Guy threw his head back and laughed, then shook her hand. "In two weeks; I'll send you the details. Also, I need to thank you for what you did earlier for my wife and me and all those frenzied kids. You saved our Christmas party. Your cookies are a hit every year, but bringing your friend over to play Santa? *Very* classy touch."

"It was my pleasure," she said, the double meaning bringing with it a bite of longing. "I'm really glad you didn't have to cancel."

Guy turned his head just then like he was looking for someone. "Speaking of your friend Santa, do you know where James went? I'd like to thank him again."

She felt her forehead pinch. "I'm not sure. He's not... He didn't come with me tonight."

Now Guy's forehead was the one that narrowed in confusion. "Huh. That's odd." He quickly scanned the room. "I could have sworn I saw him by the tree. But it's Christmas Eve. I guess it must have been someone else dressed up like Santa."

* * *

Guy went to speak to another guest and Anna couldn't help it—she looked beyond the big tree toward the doorway. Sure enough, a man in a Santa suit and long white wig was walking away.

If it really was him, she could run after him, tell him to stay, that together they would figure things out. Learn to risk their vulnerable hearts again and open up. To trust.

No! Not doing that.

She had been right to listen to her instinct about him leaving because it was playing out before her eyes. *Come on, Anna, what more do you need to see?* There he goes, walking out the door, never to look back.

Her legs seemed to have other ideas, however, because she hurried to the back of the room.

But then she got her big girl panties on properly straight and stopped herself, almost skidding to a halt before she reached the tree. *What are you running toward? Deceit and hurt, once again?*

Besides, it might not even be him. Although from the man's stature, his gait, and what she already knew in her heart, it was.

All afternoon, she had been giving herself reasons not to get involved, but what if she looked at the upside? What if, just for argument's sake, she gave in to their incredible chemistry and the pleasure, loosely defined, of having him to spend time with? He might not stay here forever, but, okay, long distance, couldn't they figure that out?

Of course they could.

What she feared the most wasn't that he might physically move away but that he would suddenly retreat from their relationship. Blindside her with little warning, come home one day and simply say, *Anna, it's over. I'm done.*

For example.

But that fear grew out of her old relationship with Blake, and if she were going to look toward the future, she would have to be braver than avoidance.

She thought back to her first impression of James this morning, in that split second of stop-motion time before she processed that he had crashed into her boxes with his Santa belly and that her cookies were falling.

That first impression told her he was a man with a twinkle in his eyes that said presence, and then later he became the man who gave her sugar, and the one who knocked at the bakery's back door wanting to help her. He was the man who made her laugh in the car and who was such an amazing kisser.

And here, tonight, James was the man who showed up.

That didn't change the fact that—she looked toward the door again to confirm—his back was to her because he was leaving, that was clear.

Or was he?

In that instant he stopped as if he heard her thoughts, paused mid-step, turned around, and with a determined walk, came back in. When he looked up and saw her watching him, he stopped suddenly and smiled, a relieved but tentative look.

He closed the distance between them fast. "Anna."

"What are you doing here?" *No.* What she meant was, "Why were you leaving?"

"I'm sorry," he said, shaking his head, the curls from his Santa wig wagging. "My brain got all muddled. I decided to come here to tell you...a few things. But then I got scared, and I also thought you might not want me here. First, I was standing, hiding, behind the tree, and then I told myself I should leave. But on my way out the door, I knew I had to come back." He chuckled sheepishly, narrowed his eyes, shook his head again like he knew it didn't make a whole lot of sense.

At the same time, they both reached for the other's hands as if they had done it many times before.

He let out a heavy breath. "The first thing I have to tell you is," he paused to weave his fingers between hers. His palms were warm and soft but also strong. "Congratulations on being chosen and even more congratulations on telling them no. That was a kick-ass speech. When I heard you say that stuff, I did a fist bump in the air. I almost knocked an ornament off the tree."

"You would have blown your cover because, given how we met, I would have guessed it was you causing the ruckus." His eyes, that smile, the laughter, they were magnetic, and they drew her gaze to his. "What else were you going to tell me?" she asked.

"That you were right, I was considering leaving, moving away. I interviewed for another job a few weeks ago. In the past five years, I haven't stayed anywhere more than four or five months, and I was starting to get restless. Tonight after you left my place, the headhunter I've been working with called and told me I got it. It's in Portland and she said there's a housing subsidy and a rental with a view of the river."

"You're speaking in present tense, and you said I was right so I guess this means you're going."

So much for looking at the positives, for being willing to open her heart again, for pushing herself to start trusting.

He squeezed her hands tighter in his. "I turned it down. I'm not going anywhere, Anna."

It wasn't only air from breathing in that filled her chest, it was a feeling. An expansive, happy feeling.

"I like it here, and I'm tired of roaming from place to place," he explained. "The problem isn't external; there's nothing wrong with anywhere I've been or any of the jobs I've held. The feeling of emptiness, of a void, of always looking for something that's not there? I know it was coming from me. Not to put any pressure on you—really, I'm not—but meeting you today has led me to think about staying and what might come next."

He squeezed her hands as if to emphasize what he was about to say. "I want to create a life for myself that's full, that provides some kind of belonging. Just to be clear, I'd like you to be part of that, but I'm not staying for you. If we're going to spend more days together, which I really want, I need to have my act together. For myself and also, I want to offer you a man that's whole."

Chapter 14
first date

I t felt so freeing to figure this out and to share it with someone else.

Not anyone; Anna.

Like he finally shoved the bolder off his chest that had isolated him for so long.

She stroked the top of his hands with her thumbs. Her response was like icing on an airy cake, and it made him feel even better: "James, I'd like to spend more days together too."

"What if we start tonight—what if we stay for the rest of the dinner and some dancing? Consider it our first official date since we're both...you know, here." *WTF, man, why so awkward?* "And"—he glanced downward at his costume, no longer feeling less-than because he wasn't wearing a tux— "we're both dressed up. I have a couple of hours free before I have to collect the reindeer from the bar and fire up the sleigh."

The sound of her laughter, how her smile brightened her face, he got the strangest feeling, like his legs were about to melt. "I'm not really hungry right now," she said, "I'm still shaking from my impromptu rejection speech, but I would love to dance."

"Follow me, milady." He offered his elbow and led her away from where they stood by the tree to the center of the room and onto the crowded dance floor. Who knew angel investors liked to boogie to remade Christmas carols?

He had left the white gloves and belly padding at the apartment because he was in such a hurry to get here, and now he was thankful he wasn't wearing any barrier between him and Anna. They stood so close, almost their whole bodies touched, from their chests to their thighs and, occasionally as they danced, when the sides of their calves brushed.

He felt electrified.

That word, the sensation, reminded him of the power outage, which had felt at the time like a bad omen, although maybe it actually wasn't. Anyway, he challenged himself to come up with synonyms for the feeling.

Like, hopeful, alive.

"What you told the Christmas Angels about growing slowly over time, it makes so much sense. And, Anna, I want you to know that if you'll accept my help, I would love to be part of it. I usually start work early at the hospital so I'm off by mid-afternoon. I could come by then and help with whatever you need—baking, deliveries, a sounding board for business planning. We already know we make a good team."

"That we do," she agreed. "I couldn't have done it today without your help—or your sugar donation."

"Once you find the right space, I can help with renovations; I can build your island. I'm very good with my hands."

"I am sure you are," she teased, moving her hips closer to him. He wondered if it was on purpose or, the option he preferred, unconscious.

As they swayed together silently, the hand he had around her back, he moved it so he could hold the side of her face. Her eyes closed, her shoulders relaxed, the muscles under his hand by her jaw softened.

"My attraction to you goes deeper than appearances," he said, "so don't take this the wrong way but, you look absolutely stunning tonight."

"Thank you," she whispered, tilting her face against his palm. "You know, in the shop when we kissed, you were wearing jeans and a T-shirt. I felt your stubble under my fingertips." She stroked his smooth cheek when she said that, and two things happened: He instantly felt it a couple of stories below, and he regretted having shaved. "You're a gorgeous man but I'm having a hard time reconciling, because right now you look a few decades too old for me and a bit too much like Santa."

He grabbed the wig and unstrapped it, tossed it to the edge of the dance floor, where one of the ladies wolf-whistled and shouted, "Santa, take it off!"

"Uh-oh," Anna said with a grin that made him warm. "This crowd might get wild. But I have an idea. What do you say, if the wind has calmed down, we sneak out of here and go to Crystal Cove after all, for a moonlight Christmas Eve picnic with takeout tacos?"

* * *

With two small white bags of tacos from *Achiote* in hand, because Paloma had gone home, they tromped past the historic cottages with retro decorations in the windows and onward to the beach. Anna carried her sandals with the heel straps hanging on two fingers, and the old sweatshirt she wore over her evening gown, the one she found crumpled in the back of the van, got a few smiles from the people who were leaving.

The beach was quiet; it looked like the two of them would be alone. Ironically, a gentle wisp of breeze purred in the cool air, bringing the scent of wood smoke and the ocean. The sapphire sky held twinkling stars. The curved wedge of waxing moon shined bright. From tip-top to the bottom, decorations adorned the Christmas tree on the beach, its branches lit in golden lights.

"Hey, look," she pointed off in the distance, "the faint silhouette, it's Catalina Island." The waves crashed and retreated, giving the sand a sugary, moonlit glaze. Tomorrow, she would start toying with designs for a Crystal Cove cookie for next year, a green Christmas tree on a golden beach, blue water fanning out behind it.

She got her phone out of her bag, took a picture of the tree, and texted it to the kids. Three hours ahead, they would probably still be at their concert and game and after-party meet-and-greets. She was happy they didn't feel the need to text her all the time, and although the ache of missing them pulsed in her chest, it was good for them to be spending time with their father.

And Madison.

Anna took a deep breath. An unusually deep breath. Because, she realized as she reached the end of the exhale, she was just so tired of all the bitterness and acrimony.

"That was a big sigh," James said, turning to look at her. "Care to share?"

"I guess I'm coming to a realization."

"Oh, yeah? What's that?"

"I need to start relating differently to Blake—I'm sick of always feeling on edge and resentful and expecting a fight. Everything that's happened today has me excited about going forward. I can honestly say, I want to be done looking back."

James smiled like he understood exactly what she meant, which she knew he did. "That's great, Anna, it sounds like a big milestone. It won't be easy, but it seems like an important part of healing, of...relearning how to *be* in your life." He stopped walking, closed his eyes, and hummed, *Ommm*, just for a second.

"You know, that sounds *exactly* like something my mother would have said."

He laughed at that, looked up at her with those very nice eyes of his, and spoke just two words that instantly warmed her with comfort and connection: "She did."

* * *

It made him feel like a million bucks, being able to share something Lucy had said—*now* he felt comfortable calling Dr. Washingtonn by her first name—with Anna, something that clearly made her relax, maybe even...happy.

She stopped again, held up her phone, and started a new text. He watched from beside her, curious to see what she would write.

Hi. The kids seem like they're having a great time in New York with you and Madison. I wish you two a very Merry Christmas, Blake. -A.

She looked up at James, raised her eyebrows—*here goes*—and tapped send.

He touched the back of her arm and gestured to a piece of driftwood near the shore that the waves had weathered smooth. "Table for two, milady. Shall we have a seat?"

They sat and unpacked their tacos, but before they started to eat, he lifted his drink cup, held the paper straw in place with his finger, and lightly tapped hers. "To milestones," he said. She repeated after him, and they ate their tacos and talked, mostly about nothing, which felt like everything.

Once they finished, they crumpled up the wrappers and napkins and put them back in the bag to carry out their trash. He turned to face her and felt that funny feeling in his chest again as he noticed how her eyes reflected the moonlight and the stars.

"Still hate Christmas?" he asked, putting his arm around her shoulder to give her a squeeze and draw her close.

She giggled—an actual giggle—and shook her head. He liked that she appreciated his weird sense of humor. "I told you, I don't hate..." She stopped, and he felt himself grinning, because he could tell this time, she was going to play along. "No, James. I no longer hate Christmas."

He slapped his leg, the baggy Santa pants still on. "Yes! I'm glad to hear that. Maybe my work here is done."

She shook her head, feigned a face that said he was wrong. "I don't think your work is done."

"No?" He barely contained his smile because again he guessed where she was going.

"No." And with that she moved toward him, and he kissed her again, and it was not a peck on the cheek.

When she trailed her fingers along his jaw, it gave him the shivers. Her lips, her mouth, her hunger—their exploration was more inquisitive and sensual than before.

They paused after a moment. He couldn't speak for her but he needed to catch his breath, because these sensations were bordering on overpowering.

He pressed his forehead to hers, and she closed her pretty eyes. "Were you really planning to watch a movie tonight after the gala?" he whispered. "Before we, um, bumped into each other this morning?"

It was so uncanny how familiar things felt between them, as if they'd known each other a long while.

"Yes, that was my plan, to watch a Christmas romance. Why are you asking?"

"I have an idea." He squeezed her hand, brought it to his mouth, and kissed it. "We could watch together. You can pick the movie."

She outlined his lips with her fingertip, and he put his arm around her shoulders again. "I don't think I want to watch a movie later after all," she said, tipping her head toward his and looking him in the eye.

"No?"

"A movie would be so...last year. But James, would you come home with me?"

He didn't answer her exactly but instead kissed her once more in a way that would let her know his answer was a wholehearted—a whole-bodied—*yes*.

"I'm glad we met," he said softly a moment later when they moved apart. "It feels like a long time ago already, doesn't it?"

"Mm, yes, it really does," she said, tasting his lips again.

They kissed some more and the sounds around them faded, quieter and quieter, like waves receding from the shore. Or maybe it was where his attention was focused, more on Anna's lips than on the squawking seagull, the clanking dishes in a nearby cottage, the gust of wind, or the car door in the distance slamming.

* * *

The wind gusted again, the top of the Christmas tree swayed, and a faint, far-away voice tickled her ear. "Not those winds again," she said, suddenly unsettled. "Maybe this is our sign to leave."

He pulled her closer with one arm, smoothed her blowing hair with his other hand. "It's such a nice evening otherwise, though," he replied, "and we have all night. Let's give it a minute. It's been on and off all day as you know, so I bet it might stop as fast as it started. But take it from me, to avoid getting sand in them, you should definitely close your eyes."

She lowered her lids and nestled against his side, wrapped her dress tight around her legs, dipped her head to rest on his shoulder. "You're right. It *is* a perfect night. We can wait out a little wind."

Especially when the luscious kissing started up again.

The wind blew some more, and the lights against the ornaments on the tree made a tinkling sound, and a flutter of recognition teased.

When the gusting stopped and the tree stilled, the

sounds in the distance — the footsteps in the sand, the voice growing louder calling *Mom! Mom!* — made Anna spin around.

Carli was running toward them.

Anna jumped up and caught her in a hug, "Oh, my goodness, what are you doing here!?"

James rose too and stood by Anna's side just as Ben and Blake caught up.

Quickly Anna made introductions. Blake shook James' hand and glanced at the Santa suit. His eyes darted to Anna trying to figure out what was going on, and then refocusing, he nodded to Carli. "Carl, why don't you explain it to your mom?"

Carli held up a fist and turned it, and at first Anna wasn't sure what that meant but then she realized Carli was showing off her wrist.

The wrist without a Spiralo watch.

"I changed my mind about the watch, and we didn't go to the concert or the Buckets' game." She looked down at the sand and then back up at Anna. "I missed you, Mom. And Ben did too—he hasn't been home since the summer. We asked Dad if we could trade our gifts for plane tickets instead. It was *so* last minute, but"—Carli looked at Blake adoringly, and for a welcome change that pleased Anna unconditionally—"he was on the phone with the airline for like forever, but he was able to get us the last three seats. Maddy agreed to fly home alone tomorrow instead."

"Oh, sweetie. This is The. Very. Best. Christmas. Present. Hashtag *ever*."

"Okay, Mom, don't be a dork." Over Carli's head Anna whispered *thank you* to Blake.

He nodded once, *you're welcome*, and held up his phone. "I just saw your text. I really appreciate that, Anna."

"How did you find me?" she asked.

"You weren't at the house or the bakery, and when Carli mentioned your contest thing, we also went to the country club. The kids said they were here with you a couple of Christmas eves ago, so we figured we would try here next."

Anna hugged Ben. She was surprised he hadn't chosen to stay in New York to spend the time with friends. "How long are you home?"

"A week." That was his man-of-few-words way, but his being here said much more.

"That's amazing, sweetie. What a treat. I thought I wouldn't see you until February break."

"Mom!" Clearly Carli was excited; she was speaking in exclamation points. "How did it go with the Christmas Angels?"

"Good. I mean, I won. And then they gave a summary of their ideas for changes we could make, and after that, I said no. No, thank you. Politely."

Blake cocked an eyebrow at that, gave her an *are you serious?* look. Carli already was scrolling and holding up her phone. "The video of you is all over social media, Mom!" Blake and Ben moved in to see Carli's screen and Anna felt reassured of her decision as their eyes all widened at the same time.

"Wow, Mom. You're gonna have a line out the door the day after Christmas," Carli said.

"Yeah, she's going to be too busy to take you clothes shopping," Ben teased.

Anna felt someone looking at her, and she glanced up to find an unfamiliar expression on Blake's face. She could tell that, for the first time in many, many years, he might be seeing her differently.

In addition to being Anna, his kids' difficult mother and

his endlessly harping ex-wife, she guessed he now also saw Anna the business owner, the mom his kids wanted to come home to, the confident woman in her own right—who also happened to have a sexy man by her side, even if he was dressed like Santa. And because Blake was Blake, and no one changes *that* much, she also guessed it might have something to do with the thigh-high slit in her dress.

James must have noticed it too, because although she couldn't imagine that he was the possessive type, he squeezed her hand a little tighter.

* * *

In person, Carli was the spitting image of Anna, only a younger, lankier teenage version. Ben had Anna's kind eyes and Blake's nose and mouth. James was thrilled for her that the kids so thoughtfully surprised her, and that Blake had made it happen. Pretty amazing.

After Anna hugged the kids, James leaned close and whispered, "I think this is my cue to leave, milady." He hated the idea of saying goodbye, especially with how her ex was looking at her. But this was her family and James wasn't part of nor could he compete with that. "I believe it's time for me to go."

She grasped him by the forearm and looked him in the eyes. "No, don't go. Please stay."

"Okay, sure."

This meant a lot, his being included, and he was honored. If they had met in some other more conventional way and been dating, he doubted she would have introduced him to her kids so soon. Even if it were Christmas.

But when Carli next spoke, her words doused James'

sudden, rosy-eyed glow. "Mom, I know it's late, but can we make Grandma's chocolate chip cookies?"

He pictured the ornament, the small Santa plate he had seen on Lucy's desk that now lived in Anna's bakery.

There would be no way Anna would say no to baking her mother's cookies with her kid on Christmas Eve, and he did not blame her in the slightest. It wasn't every day your fifteen-year-old asked for some of your time.

Sure enough, Anna was looking at him with regret in her eyes, a furrowed brow, and a head tilt that said, *on second thought I'm sorry.*

Blake looked between her and James, coughed, and then piped up. "Hey Carl, why don't you, uh, make them at my place? I haven't had them in years and I'm sure Maddy would love to taste them when she gets home in the morning."

Carli looked at him like he was stupid. "She doesn't eat any sugar, Dad. Or flour."

James would have laughed at that—if he weren't about to cry.

"I'm sure she'll make an exception," Blake said, "and if not, I'll eat her share."

"But I want to stay at Mom's tonight," Carli said. "That's why we came home—to spend Christmas with her."

James caught Ben, too, glancing between him and Anna, old enough to get what was going on. He stepped forward, threw his arm around his sister's shoulders. "Come on Carl, Mom must be sick of baking cookies right now, and you're right, it's late, really late"—he glanced at James. "I want some of Grandma's cookies too. Let's make them at Dad's."

"Your brother's right, I could use a break from baking

tonight," Anna told her, "but how about if we make a batch tomorrow?"

Carli acquiesced to that plan, and now Anna was again saying *thank you* over her head to Blake. Which meant everyone was cool, Blake was taking the kids home.

"See you guys tomorrow. Call me when you want me to pick you up," Anna said, before hugging Ben first and then Carli.

When they were married, Blake had made Anna feel small and unseen and abandoned, so James did not like him from the get-go. But he was her kids' father, and he had just stepped up so she could have some alone time with James. Who had been lucky enough to kiss her many times today. He decided to take the high road.

While Blake watched Anna say goodnight to the kids, James took a few steps closer and extended his hand once more. "Very nice to meet you, Blake, and Merry Christmas to you and your wife."

For some reason, this seemed to stump Blake, who looked like he didn't know what to say. "Thanks, same to you. Merry Christmas," he stammered back. "Anna, you and"—he looked James up and down again—"Santa, you two have a good night."

* * *

Once she and James were alone on the beach, they kissed some more, and then they drove to her condo. He stood beside her while she put her key into the front door lock, her hands quivering with nerves and anticipation. But her nervousness didn't last long because he looked up toward the roof of her building and said with all seriousness, "Hold on, Anna. I'll meet you inside—tonight I should use the chimney."

She lost track of how many times he had made her laugh today. It felt good. Warm and welcome and...just plain nice.

She sent him to the living room to take a seat on the couch while in the kitchen she poured them glasses of eggnog. When she returned and he joked that she should sit on Santa's lap to tell him what she wanted, she climbed onto his legs and did just that.

"Okay, then, if you insist," he teased. He lifted the sweat-shirt off her, and with his finger traced the strap of her dress before moving it off her shoulder. The sensation on her skin of the fabric drifting over it and his fingertips trailing behind made her shiver. "Are you cold?" he asked in between kisses and undressing her. "Because I can lend you my Santa coat."

She loved how he could be funny and thrill her body at the same time. "That's alright." The smile on her lips faded. "Let's go to bed instead."

Their eggnog sat un-drunk on the side table, and her Christmas romances paled in comparison to her real-life day today—more importantly, to James. He was sexy and he smelled good, and she would not waste a second staring at some screen even if he were beside her watching it too.

Once in her bedroom and relieved of her gown, she slipped under the covers and watched as he undressed. First the costume and then his everyday clothes, and then she gazed at his exquisite body before he climbed into bed beside her. When he took her in his arms, it felt tender and also stimulating.

He wore no goofy elf hat like the studly rink attendant in her dream. No jingle bells jangled as he deliciously kissed his way down her body. Her self-consciousness melted away, and it seemed like his did too. Just like at the bakery this afternoon, she didn't have to provide much direction; he knew *exactly* what to do. Although it was Christmas Eve and not the Fourth of July, fireworks burst in the sky. (Okay, not quite.) The sex was in a word amazing.

Spiced with laughter.

Passionate.

And dirty.

When they took a break, she snuggled close to him and rested her head on his shoulder, while her heart rested assured that with him it was safe.

"What you said earlier, about helping me at the bakery, I'd like that," she told him as she caressed lazy circles on his chest. "I suspect Carli was right about it being busier after we re-open, and also, you got me very excited when you said you could help build my island."

He laughed at that, accompanied by twinkling eyes she could see just fine in the darkened room. He teased about checking her excitement level and then he did and it made her moan with pleasure and she forgot what they were talking about for the next few minutes.

As her breath came back to its normal rhythm, he said, "Anna, I don't say anything I don't mean. I would love to help you. But I do have one condition."

"What might that be this time?" She managed to nudge herself up on her elbow to see him better, although her muscles still felt weak.

"On your next day off or one evening after you close the bakery, would you come shopping with me—help me pick out furniture for my place and some posters or artwork for the walls?"

"It would be my pleasure," she said. And at the word

pleasure, he reached down again to touch her. "I guess that means"—his fingers were adept, and they made her gasp mid-sentence—"you're really staying?"

"I already told you I am. Anna, I'm committed." He kissed her then at the exact same time his hand did more wonderful things that led to a third (really!) burst of fireworks. "We could also team up next Christmas, with you baking for the hospital again while I play Santa. I'm less likely to destroy your cookies if we coordinate efforts."

"Good thinking," she said, again trying to catch her breath. "I'd like that."

It sounded like the start of a tradition.

epilogue: christmas
eve one year later

The kitchen light was on when Anna crept downstairs in the dark. *That's odd.* Maybe she forgot to turn it off last night. But then something rustled, and it sounded like the coffee maker lid pressing down on a pod. She rounded the corner and there was Carli, standing at the counter. In navy-striped boxers and a pink tank top, her lanky arms danced in mid-air as she took two mugs from the upper cabinet.

"Honey, what are you doing awake? It's so early."

Carli's mussed light-brown topknot bobbed as she positioned the mugs under the spouts. "I couldn't sleep. I thought I'd make you coffee before the baking marathon. Which is it today, Sugar Cookie Light Roast, or an espresso?"

"Double shot," Anna replied, trying not to let her surprise show. Carli had matured so much over the past year. "Why do you think you can't sleep?"

"Not sure," she mumbled, turning to face the coffee maker. She seemed anxious but not in a bad way, more like excited. Anna didn't want to risk an eye roll by asking if she was jazzed about Christmas—that would be so little-kid—so instead she decided to ask, "Are you looking forward to Christmas at your dad's?"

There was no New York City extravaganza this year; Blake and Maddy were staying home. Carli didn't want to miss rehearsals for her New Year's Day violin recital, and water polo practice started the morning after. Besides, they were all going to New York in late April for Ben's graduation.

With her back to Anna, Carli shrugged. "Yeah, it should be fun. Dad said Maddy is going to cook, so...wish me luck."

Anna chuckled. From what the kids had told her, Madison was more skilled at picking up carry-out or calling the caterer. "I'm sure it'll be fine. And you like to cook—you could offer to help her out."

"I know. I already told her I'd help this afternoon. This morning I booked a practice room at the library."

"Good for you," Anna said, trying not to let her swelling pride at Carli's adulting show. "Your solo is going to be great next week, and I'm sure Maddy will appreciate the support."

With a hiss and a trickle, the wondrous smell of coffee filled the kitchen. Carli reached for one of the mugs. "Actually, wait," she said, leaving it in place. From the dish drainer beside the sink, she removed the tall metal travel cup, poured the coffee into it, screwed on the cover, and gave it, somewhat unsteadily, to Anna.

"Thanks, kiddo. You okay?"

"I'm good," Carli answered briskly. "You need to get going, Mom, it's almost four o'clock."

* * *

Now that the deliveries with Santa were done, James swept the back room a final time while Anna finished wiping down the counters, before quickly changing into her gown.

They drove to the country club and just outside the double wooden doors, James tugged on the hand of hers he had been holding. When she turned to face him, he asked, "Are you sure about this—are you sure I'm dressed appropriately?"

Right before Halloween, he asked her to take him shopping for a tuxedo, but she consulted with Guy who agreed with her: James playing Santa was a tradition the O.C. Christmas Angels should hold on to.

"Yes," she said as she stood up on her toes to kiss him. "Yes, I'm sure. You're perfect."

As the new emcee, Anna left him sitting at their table and she climbed the stairs to the stage. After sharing the news that Guy had decided to retire early, she led the crowd in a round of applause. The five contestants took turns introducing themselves, and then she said a few words before announcing this year's winner. Unlike last year, the recipient of the Angels' investment was thrilled to accept their venture backing.

When her official duties as gala host were over, James led her to the dance floor.

"You were magnificent, milady. I'm very impressed with your leadership skills. And," he lowered his voice to a whisper that brushed her neck, "I have some skills of my own I'd like to share."

"I'm so looking forward to your skills later. It feels like we haven't spent the night together in forever."

Call Anna old fashioned but if Carli was in the house, Anna wasn't yet okay with James sleeping over. Between their work hours, the new bakery renovation, and Carli's unpredictable schedule that made it impossible to know when she would pop home, it had been a very long time.

"You're telling me," he said, tenderly holding the side of her face. "But first, I want to show you the drawings for your island. *Islands*, plural. I took another look and the way I've configured things, I think we can squeeze in two."

She pictured the second location and the New Year's Day opening, only a week away. The sweet one-story Craftsman bungalow had been for sale, at a good price because it needed TLC. But even at that, and even if she rented out half, it was still more than she could afford.

After several conversations about how she and James would renovate, the owner agreed to lease it to her. It was located off the main shopping street but in a cluster of busy establishments, and if business at her original shop kept up its pace, she could afford the rent.

They had been renovating for months now, it felt like every spare minute, and James was proving even more than she already knew just how good he could be with his hands. All that was left now other than a flurry of email and social media marketing was construction of her marble-topped island—or according to James now, two.

"What if you show me the drawings after?" She slipped her hand between the buttons on his Santa jacket to rub his chest. "Hey, are you okay? Your heart's beating really fast."

He took hold of her wrist and moved her hand away. "I'm fine, just getting excited about later. About what happens *after* I show you the drawings."

"Well, then." She looked up at his handsome face. "They don't need me here anymore. Why don't we take off?"

He didn't wait to answer, just danced her off the

parquet floor in the center of the room with his thigh discreetly, suggestively nudged between her legs.

They stopped at their seats so she could grab her purse, and they headed for the door. Just as she was getting into the passenger side of James' car, her phone vibrated against her hip from inside her bag.

He got in and watched her check it while he started the engine. "It's Carli," she said before reading the string of texts out loud.

> I don't feel good.

> I think I'm getting sick. Two kids in my biology class had the flu last week.

> Maybe I caught it.

"Emojis," Anna narrated. "The green face, the one with the mask, the one with the thermometer dangling from the mouth."

> Dad's bringing me home soon.

> I want to sleep in my own bed.

Anna typed back...

> We're leaving the gala right now. I'll meet you at home.

She didn't have the heart to say, *Please, pretty please, do you think you could not feel good at your dad's house tonight instead?*

As soon as she sent her reply, she turned to James. "I

don't want to leave her home alone if she's getting sick or for you to catch it and also—"

"I know," he said, his expression a mix of concern and disappointment. "No sleepovers when she's home. I'll drop you off and head back to the apartment."

"I'm sorry." Anna started to feel bad about him spending the night alone, Christmas Eve of all nights, but then her mind flashed back exactly one year ago. When she had gone with him to his place to change into her gala dress, that sad, empty apartment had almost scared her away.

Since then, they had totally turned it around. They had shopped for comfortable furniture—two deep chairs and a cozy sectional—and a large flat-screen TV. Two nice area rugs, artwork and some photographs—including a bitter-sweet one of little Noah grinning—on freshly painted walls.

After Thanksgiving, they got him a Christmas tree from a local farm, bought boxes of lights and decorations, and Anna gave him her mother's Christmas cookie plate ornament.

"Don't apologize. I understand, I just hope it's nothing serious. As for me, at least I'll get a full night's sleep," he teased.

* * *

After he dropped Anna off at her condo, James drove around the corner and parked at the end of a cul-de-sac, beyond the last street light. He cut the engine, turned off the lights, rested his hands on the top of the steering wheel, and let out a ginormous sigh. The tension had been building all night—compounded by how hard he tried not to let it show—and soon it would finally be time.

epilogue: christmas eve one year later

His phone simultaneously beeped and buzzed, and he grabbed it from the center console.

> Almost there. We'll flash the lights when we turn the corner.

He texted back a thumbs-up.

Then because he was so antsy and needed to move, he got out of his car and went to the trunk to quadruple-check. Yes, there they were, the drawings for her island and, more importantly, the small red box.

A car slowed near the corner and its blinker went on but no headlights flashed, so he knew it wasn't them. *Breathe, man. Give them a second.*

He watched it turn and realized there was another car coming down the street behind it. The blinker went on, and as the vehicle slowed, the headlights, they flashed!

Excitement squeezed his chest, making his heart pump even faster.

Only a few more minutes now.

He got back into the car so as not to arouse the neighbors' suspicion and tried to do that almost-impossible thing he and Anna learned in last month's meditation workshop, where you focus on nothing else but your breath.

A few minutes later, his phone beeped and buzzed again.

> I'm in.

He laughed at that, like she had gotten past some high-security institution's alarm system.

> Told her I want to watch one of her happy-ever-after Christmas movies.

epilogue: christmas eve one year later

She just went upstairs to change.

Door unlocked.

I'm in living room.

He texted the thumbs up again, turned off the sound on his phone, and watched as the car that had dropped her off came back around the corner. This time it turned in James' direction and parked across the street. James gave a peace-sign wave to Blake.

Time to spring into action. James blew out a short, hard breath through pursed lips and jumped out, gathered the drawings and the box, and pressed the fob to lock the car. He nodded at Blake, who lowered his window and called out, "Good luck."

Careful not to crush the drawings and with a pat to confirm yet again that the box was safely tucked in his pocket, James ran around the corner and down the street to Anna's condo.

As planned, he stayed quiet when he got there, tiptoeing along the outside wall by her patio door, next to the clay pot and trellis of bougainvillea.

He stood still and a few minutes went by that felt like an hour, and then his phone buzzed again.

I just asked for IC.

The kid was good. Everything according to plan, exactly like they talked about, down to the strategic ice cream abbreviation. "We won't have much time," Carli had told him last week. "If she thinks I'm sick, she won't leave me alone for a second."

She went to kitchen.

At freezer.

Getting bowls out of cabinet = noise

Now spoons. Go!

Here goes. He opened the back door as quietly as he could and slipped inside.

Carli must have leapt off the couch because she immediately met him in the short hallway and followed him toward the kitchen. His heart... holy cow. The fast pulse Anna noticed earlier? That was nothing compared to how it raced now.

* * *

Carli let herself into the house a few minutes after Anna, who was boiling water for tea in the kitchen. "Come here, Honey," she said as she put her lips to Carli's forehead. "You don't feel warm, that's good."

Carli coughed and sniffled. "I can't get sick, Mom. The recital..."

"Let's not get ahead of ourselves. It's a week away. If you have a cold, you should be fine by then. Go, get your PJs on and get ready for bed. Whatever you're coming down with, you'll need your rest."

"But I'm not really tired, and it's Christmas Eve. Could we watch one of your Christmas movies together?"

"Oh, no. You must be seriously ill if you want to see one of those," Anna deadpanned. Carli usually made fun of her for watching what she called Anna's sappy movies.

Carli tilted her head and chuckled, then coughed. "I know, right? Don't tell anyone. But really, Mom, can we watch one?"

Anna hesitated. She did not want Carli to get the idea that real life was like some fairy tale TouchingHearts network movie. But maybe this was her way of trying to connect. If she wanted to watch a TouchingHearts Christmas movie, who was Anna to say no?

"Sure, we can. I'm just going to change out of my dress, and I'll be right down. I'll meet you on the couch."

Anna ran up the stairs and put on her softest yoga pants and one of James' gray T-shirts, which she had worn home from his place last weekend. She unpinned her updo, brushed out her hair, twisted it up, and clipped it.

In the living room, she sat down next to Carli and, with the remote, scanned the guide for a movie she had seen already, one she knew was the least fantastical and unreal.

She looked over at Carli, who was hugging a pillow to her body, tense. "Does your stomach hurt?"

"No, I just feel....I don't know." She sniffled and coughed again. "My throat is a little sore."

Anna felt her forehead again. "Cool as a cucumber. I definitely don't think you have fever. My guess is, it's a cold. Do you think some ice cream would help your throat?"

"Mm, I think it might."

Anna chuckled. Carli might be maturing fast, but she still had childlike moments that Anna relished.

She had been so busy lately with the bakery renovation and getting the Christmas orders ready that she suspected Carli was less sick than in need of some relaxed one on one time with her mother.

"You're in luck, kiddo—I think we still have some BFB in

the house. Be right back." Anna got up and went to the kitchen, took out the pint of Balboa Frozen Banana she kept on hand, then to the cabinet to get two bowls. As she closed the cabinet door, she swore she heard the back door slide open and closed.

"Carl?" she called.

And then it sounded like a man's voice.

Was someone in the house!?

"Carli!" she yelled as she dropped the ice cream container in the sink and reached for a knife from the block on the counter. "Are you alright?"

"I'm fine, Mom," she called from the hall. "Everything's fine, just calm down."

"She's fine." It was a man's voice. James' voice.

He stood in the archway to the kitchen, Carli coming up behind him, a funny look on her face.

"What's going on?" Anna wanted to know, exhaling with relief as she put the knife down. He was still wearing his Santa suit. "I'm happy to see you, but I thought we agreed..."

James cleared his throat. "About the plans I wanted to talk to you about..." From behind him, Carli made a sound like a squeal and then she clapped her hand over her mouth. James was holding the rolled-up drawings of her islands and from the way the paper jittered, she could tell his hand was shaking.

"Are you okay? What's wrong?"

"Anna." His voice cracked, and he cleared his throat again. "Anna. About plans, I have to ask you something."

"Of course." She reached for his empty hand in an effort to calm him. "What is it?" But instead of answering her or taking the hand she offered, he reached into his pocket and got down on one knee in front of her.

It took a beat for what he was doing to sink in. *Could he be?*

He set down the drawings on the floor beside him, and she could see he was holding a tiny box. "Anna," he started, looking up at her with those eyes of his. "We met last Christmas Eve, and we've been together for exactly one year. I know in the grand scheme of things that's not such a long time, but I want you to know, I need you to know, that of anything in my entire life, I have never been so sure. I love you, and I know because of what happened in the past you'll want to take this slow, but I hope... Would you consider getting married again? Not getting married again to anyone, I mean. Anna, lovely Anna, at whatever point in time you feel ready, will you marry *me*?"

Her vision blurred from the pooling tears. It was the sweetest, most sincere proposal she could have imagined. Not that she had imagined this moment. He was right—in the scheme of things, their time together had been short, but they often talked about how destined their meeting seemed, how natural their relationship felt, and all the things they wanted to do, as if it was a given they would share a future. They talked about big things, like new locations for the bakery and vacations they dreamt of taking, alone and with the kids. And they also talked about more modest, mundane things—what beach they would go to on their next day off and what they would make for dinner.

She looked at the man kneeling in front of her, with his bright eyes and the way he tilted his head like he did when he was flustered, one of the many adorable and earnest mannerisms she loved. Sensitivity and affection, humor and so much caring—he, their relationship, had helped to quiet that voice in her head, the one that for so long reminded her it was safer to go it alone.

James helped her let her guard down through so many small and not-so-small gestures; he helped her relearn what it felt like to trust. He was committed, even before the proposal—she knew that in her heart and she also knew, so was she.

Behind him Carli was bouncing up and down with excitement and holding up her phone. Anna could see a grinning Ben on the screen, also watching them.

She pulled James up so he was standing. "Yes," she said as she leaned up on her toes to kiss him. It was slow and soft and loving, and she would have continued for a long time if she hadn't remembered the kids. "Yes, I want to marry you."

"Okay, good." He pretended to wipe sweat from his brow.

She laughed yet again at his quirky, endearing humor and gave him one more kiss, this time a quick one. "I love you."

"James," Carli whispered from behind him, still bouncing, "open the box."

"Right." He turned around to her and said, "Thanks, Coach."

"So, Anna, about the ring. If what I'm about to show you doesn't work for any reason, we'll get a new one. I, I mean, we—me and your kids—we thought this would be the right choice. But there was a theft of sorts involved in procuring it, and so as I said, if it's not right, we'll fix it."

Theft? What? Before she could grasp what he meant, he opened the box to reveal a cushion of velvet and tucked into it, her mother's engagement ring.

"Her ring. How did you..." She looked up at Carli whose expression was frozen in sheepishness and excitement, both.

"I did the thieving, Mom. James told Ben and me that

he wanted to propose—*if* we were cool with it, which we so are—and he asked what style ring we thought you would like. I knew you kept Grandma's rings in the jewelry box on your dresser, and I gave the engagement ring to him for you; we thought it would be extra special."

"It's perfect," Anna said as she wiped away the tear that had started down her face. Then from the box she took the ring. Now it was her hand that shook, and James took it from her and slid it on her finger. Then he gave her the briefest yet most loving kiss.

He pulled away, cleared his throat, and gave Carli a knowing look and a subtle thumbs up.

"So you two were in on this?" Anna asked Carli and looked at Ben on the phone.

Just then someone knocked on the front door. "I'll get it!" Carli said, taking off to go open it. She was back in a flash with Blake coming up behind her, holding a bottle of champagne with a gold ribbon tied at the neck.

"Congratulations, Anna, and congratulations, James." He handed her the bottle and glanced at her left hand. "I'm happy for you." He looked at the floor and up at Anna again. "Madison and I are happy for you."

"Come on, Dad, let's go," Carli said and turned toward Anna. "I'm going back to Dad's so you and James can spend your Christmas Eve–engagement night alone."

Anna stared at her daughter. Now things were coming together. "You're not sick."

"I'm not sick." She hugged Anna. "This is good, Mom. I'm happy for you too, happy for all of us." She and James high-fived, and Ben told Anna he would call her tomorrow. And then they were gone; the house was quiet.

James wrapped his arms around Anna's waist, kissed the top of her head, and rested his chin there. "I was so nervous. It's good I don't have to do that every day. In fact, lovely Anna, I plan never to do it again. I hope I wasn't too awkward."

She took hold of the lapels of his Santa coat and drew him even closer. "I love you, James. I want to marry you. You weren't awkward; for me, you're perfect."

* * *

Thank you for reading! For more Anna and James, download the companion Reading & Book Club Guide at my website (talyablaine.com).

If you're so moved, please consider leaving a review on social media, your fave retailer or book review website, your own blog or podcast. Each review or IRL mention to a friend or relative really makes a difference.

Last but not least, if you'd like to stay updated on new releases, head to my website and join my email list.

a note from the author

Thank you for reading *Santa and Anna Christmas Cookie Crash*! This novel was inspired by a short story I wrote, called "Santa & Anna." That little story was part of a collection of five Christmas romance short stories set in the California Dreams world, and many early readers said "Santa & Anna" was their favorite piece in it. Mr. Blaine too was partial to that one, which he affectionately referred to as "the cookie story."

Although I think it's always hard for writers to choose favorites among their works, that piece spoke to me a bit more loudly than the other short stories also. I loved the protagonists, Anna and James, and it was hard to stop thinking about them—their banter, their easy way of interacting (including being quiet together), their ability to see the other's pain even when they had other pressing priorities.

I wanted to know more about the few hours they spent together at Anna's bakery on Christmas Eve: I wanted to see how their chemistry would grow. I wanted to know what they would reveal to each other that they didn't usually talk about. I wanted more of James' steadiness and quirky sense of humor.

As their attraction blossomed, I also wanted to know what would happen when their respective defenses were threatened and as their unexpected shared day came to a close. Given the way they met, it would be easy enough to go back to their "old" lives. Would they?

All of that curiosity led me to expand the short story into this novel, *Santa and Anna Christmas Cookie Crash*. I hope you enjoy reading it as much as I loved writing it!

If you're moved to leave a review—social media, book review website, your own blog or podcast—I'd so appreciate it. Each review or IRL mention to someone else really makes a difference, including to other readers.

Thank you for your support. It means the world.

XO,

Talya

About the Author

I write poignant, thought-provoking romance featuring characters over forty and swoon-worthy, "nice guy" beta heroes. My stories range from sweet(ish), closed-door romance to fogged-up doors wide open -- the characters and stories decide, me...not so much.

(📚 Hint: You'll find light, pastel covers on my closed-door stories and darker, moodier covers on the steamy ones.)

I love writing about mature people navigating romance alongside real-life issues, with all their grit and joy -- and, of course, a happy ending.

If I'm not writing or reading, I'm probably cooking, taking a walk (woods, beach, city—it's all good), or spending time with Mr. Blaine, my exceptionally funny, sweet and sexy, real-life romance hero.

You can learn more at talyablaine.com, follow me on BookBub or Goodreads, or join my email list for news of upcoming releases.

Also by Talya Blaine

CALIFORNIA DREAMS SERIES

California Dreams Christmas Romance Collection
(short stories)

"...a delightful read, perfect for the holiday season...an ideal read for a lazy afternoon." (*NetGalley reviewer*)

Spice level: 🌶️🌶️ to 🌶️🌶️🌶️ / 5

Santa and Anna Christmas Cookie Crash (a novel)

"It's warm, hopeful, and just a little bit magical, the way the best holiday stories always are." (Literary Titan)

"Sugar, spice, and everything nice are the main ingredients in this cozy holiday romance." (Publishers Weekly Booklife Prize)

Spice level: 🌶️🌶️ / 5

TRANSFORMATION SERIES

"Wow! Wow! Wow! The first truly believable BDSM series I have read...a serious, deeply sensual exploration of desire, written expertly and sensitively... These two characters have been crafted to perfection...you'll never be able to forget them." -Goodreads reviewer

Silently (Book 1)

"the new 50 Shades" (*NetGalley reviewer*)

Spice level: 🌶️🌶️🌶️🌶️ / 5

Secretly (Book 2)

Publishers Weekly BookLife Prize quarter-finalist

Spice level: 🌶️🌶️🌶️🌶️ / 5

Entirely (Book 3)

"as tender as it is steamy..." (*NetGalley reviewer*)

Spice level: 🌶️🌶️🌶️🌶️ / 5